T0064544

flip-flops

flip-flops

A Christian Fable

Written & Illustrated By:

_____

SHANAE M. GAMBLE

authorHOUSE®

AuthorHouse™
1663 Liberty Drive
Bloomington, IN 47403
www.authorhouse.com
Phone: 1 (800) 839-8640

For more information regarding permission, write to:
CHRISTIAN MYTHS AND FABLES
website: www.shanaegamble.webs.com
PO BOX 2573 Valdosta, GA 31604
This publication contains the opinion and ideas of the author. Persons or places in this
book is used for informative purposes only and not related to realistic events. It is sold with
the understanding that the publisher is not engaged in rendering psychological, medical,
or professional services. If expert assistance is needed, consult a competent professional.

Illustrated © 2015 Shanae M. Gamble

NIV
Scripture quotations marked NIV are taken from the Holy Bible, New
International Version®. NIV®. Copyright © 1973, 1978, 1984 by International
Bible Society. Used by permission of Zondervan. All rights reserved. [Biblica

KJV
Scripture quotations marked KJV are from the Holy Bible, King James Version
(Authorized Version). First published in 1611. Quoted from the KJV Classic
Reference Bible, Copyright © 1983 by The Zondervan Corporation.

Published by AuthorHouse 08/04/2015

ISBN: 978-1-5049-1271-6 (sc)
ISBN: 978-1-5049-1270-9 (e)

Print information available on the last page.

This book is printed on acid-free paper.

FLIP-FLOPS

Life with Bryson has been wonderful these past few years. I cannot believe that I could love someone this much. After having a famous mother whom I never met, days for me seem less complete. However, now I can continue the family legacy with my new upcoming gospel album, "My Love Letter to God." Grandma Susie is not as healthy as she used to be five years ago with the second breast replacement. I am just hoping she can stay around for a little while longer. I don't have any other family to rely on. Maybe the Lord will answer my prayer and restore my grandma's health. Bryson gets angry when I talk to long on my cellular. He asks why I do not use the home line. Under my breath, I just sigh as I read from Recee's old bible:

"But the Advocate, the Holy Spirit, whom the Father will send in my name, will teach you all things and will remind you of everything I have said to you. Peace I leave with you; my peace I give you I do not give to you as the world gives. Do not let your hearts be troubled and do not be afraid." (John14:26 NIV).

Dedicated to my "Besties" who inspire and encourage me in the writing process.

Acknowledgments

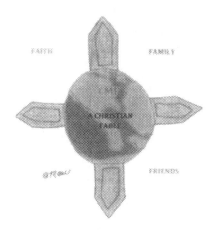

I would like to thank GOD for what He has already done in my life. He is the "cornerstone" to my existence, the truth and life, my provider, my strength, my redeemer, and my Savior. Through HIM I know all things are possible.[1]

"And we know that all things work together for good to them that love God, to them who are the called according to his purpose" Romans 8: 28 KJV[1]

Thank you, dad, Calvin Gamble, for being my foundation and the strength in my decisions. Thank you indefinitely mom, Vivian Gamble, for being my biggest cheerleader and supporter in all my ambitions and dreams.... When I give up, you don't. Thank you, sister, Regina Ogden, and big bro, Lavertt Ogden, for encouragement and looking past my flaws and loving me the same. Thank you Aunt Liz for growing seeds in CMF.... Special thanks to Mr. Chadwick D. Daniels for making life a little more simple....I love you!.....and to Saleah Tinsley and Ebonie Cohens, for those late night talks and early morning decisions.....and special thanks to all other friends, family, colleagues, and fans of CMF.... I love you dearly.

I would like to thank my pastor, James R. Carlyle, "Pastor", and First Lady, "Mrs. Angie," for being great role models and mentors in Christ throughout my Christian Walk. I love you. And, special thanks to Mizpah Baptist Church for continued open arms and warm embraces each time I enter the sanctuary.

Also, thank you to all churches throughout my walk including: Beulah Grove Baptist Church and Jacob's Well Bookstore, Pastor Sam Davis, Greater Mt. Calvary Baptist Church, Pastor Dr. Charles Vinson, Greater Ekklesia Ministries, "The GEM", Bishop Mark Smith, Union Cathedral, Bishop Wade McCrae.

I want to give special thanks to Author House and supporting staff for encouragement for excellence in all my endeavors. Also, thank you Baxley News Banner (Baxley, GA), Porter's House Parable Bookstore, Lee's Bookstore, The Mailbox Club, and South Georgia Regional Library (Valdosta, GA) for embracing CMF and your continued support.

$\mathcal{F}$lip-flops, the novel, is based on fictitious characters who are considered imperfect and hide flaws in fear of being true to themselves, switching from what's real and what's not. The book is inspired by current ideas that take away from a utopian world. Each story describes a familiar situation that is delivered by patience and faith. From the beginning of time, we, as people and Christians, forget that God loves us beyond our faults and inconsistencies; thus, making Him, GOD. The characters tell their own individual stories and their mediation comes through Pastor Marks and that said "meeting place," ......the church. Although Pastor Marks also has his own problems and tests to face, he delivers "the message" as given. This, in turns, changes the course of the story to an inspirational piece worth reading.

"All scripture is given by inspiration of God, and is profitable for doctrine, for reproof, for correction, for instruction in righteousness: That the man of God may be perfect, thoroughly furnished unto all good works" (2 Timothy 3: 16, 17 KJV).

CONTENTS

CHAPTER ONE - Introductions

RACHEL

African-American Recording Artist

Life with Bryson has been wonderful these past few years. I cannot believe that I could love someone this much. After having a famous mother whom I never met, days for me seem less complete. However, now I can continue the family legacy with my new upcoming gospel album, "My Love Letter to God."

Grandma Susie is not as healthy as she used to be five years ago with the second breast replacement. I am just hoping she can stay around for a little while longer. I don't have any other family to rely on. Maybe the Lord will answer my prayer and restore my grandma's health. Bryson gets angry when I talk to long on my cellular. He asks why I do not use the home line. Under my breath, I just sigh as I read from Recee's old bible:

> *Change begins with a "sigh." So do not hold back on your blessing and "listen."*

"But the Advocate, the Holy Spirit, whom the Father will send in my name, will teach you all things and will remind you of everything I have said to you. Peace I leave with you; my peace I give you I do not give to you as the world gives. Do not let your hearts be troubled and do not be afraid." (John14:26 NIV).

BRYSON

40-year old African-American Veteran

Roy and I have been friends since we were little boys and played together back in our hometown of Augusta, GA. As we grew up, Roy started hanging out with a different crowd at military school and getting into trouble. Later, he got kicked out of my unit and the military. I fail to realize that maybe I had something to do with it also. We both were smoking "pot" that night but only he took the blame for it; he told Captain Duke that I had just got there ..... I don't know how I will ever be able to repay him. These medals would not be on my army coat if I lived up to a dishonorable discharge almost 20 years ago. Since then, I haven't seen him in years.

Angie and I got married early and had two beautiful children, Samantha and Kyle. I love island women! I started back with the drugs slowly and then almost every day. I guess I was still grieving over the guilt of knowing I am not deserving of the military honors I have hanging over me and Angie's bed. Angie is the perfect woman because of her humbleness and intriguing dialect; but, unfortunately, she is easily influenced. Crack and Ecstasy became our morning, noon, and night meals. I lost everything--- my home with the 7 acres of land in the back. After then, I couldn't control my anger. Angie got the worst end of the stick and then sometimes both ends. She tried leaving several occasions; but I will never be separated from Samantha and Kyle as she threatens....... so I took them both legally after I got my act together.

ANGIE
Jamaican Native

Growing up poor in Jamaica and not knowing my real father, one tends to forget the true meaning of monogamy just to find a way out of the life she once had. Sometimes, I can remember the wreck my mother had after trying to rush to work after the sitter not being able to keep me at age 5 while living in Augusta. I have been in foster care since and finally on my own at age 17 with the introduction to sex and drugs. I thought that maybe when we got married things would be different. However, Bryson asked me to continue being free with our sex lives because of his love for me and that no one can fill my shoes. I had Susanne and Kyle early to full-fill my husband's wishes. I wished I had done things differently despite my circumstances and age. However, that was not enough. Now, I am fighting for full custody of my kids despite my unfortunate past mistakes. I have now been clean for 6 years and 8 days and praying for a miracle.

PASTOR MARKS

African-American Prolific Speaker

I can remember years ago asking the Lord to bring me a wife. I just finished my pastorial studies at a nearby college from St. John's Baptist Church, in which I call home. Being on the minister board for two years, the Lord spoke to me that I will be in leadership for St. John Baptist Church one day. Being a young pastor can have its advantages as well as disadvantages when looking for an ideal wife. I dated women who love the Lord and some who appear to love Him. I knew I wanted someone who was virtuous, love the Lord, and was attractive to me spiritually as well as physically. I dated selective women; but seem not to have found the "one." Christian woman can be humorous sometimes. I went out with one young lady who just finished her doctoral studies in Psychology. What attracted me to her was the anointing in her voice as she spoke at church functions, her voice spoke of meekness, virtuality, and confidence. Miss Kelly Monroe was a "firecracker," a 19 inch waist, 5 foot 5 inches in height, dressed in designer suits every Sunday, and on fire for the Lord *(Pastor Marks smiling in admiration)*. I knew she would be my wife and God didn't disagree with me.

Kelly and I were united in holy matrimony the same weekend of my ceremony to be Pastor of St. John's Baptist Church, she and I are both favored by God. Only now, the sin of gluttony is overtaking my wife physical well-being. Lord, please help me!

FIRST LADY KELLY
Latina Evangelist

I have been married to Marks years now and our anniversary is in the next couple of months. I admit.... I am not the same woman I use to be. I guess it started around age 30 when I was no longer able to have children. I never told Marks until he kept suggesting that we start a family. I was too embarrassed and ashamed to admit my wrongs. But, I knew I would have to someday. In the meantime food was my alibi.

GRANDMA SUSIE
Prayer Warrior

I took in Rachel after her mom was hospitalized for having a nervous breakdown and not being able to care for her emotionally. Receel Brown is her stage name but family calls her Recee. Recee was asked to sing in London the day before having Rachel when she was asked medically to take it easy...... she broked down.... yes broked down.... Because she love her fan base and sometimes put them first over family; Reece never left my small cabin in Stone Park; she died instantly after successfully delivering Rachel. Now, my granddaughter finally decides to marry, but; I feel uneased about the idea. My bones ache each time I talk with her on the phone as Bryson yelling in the background for her to attend to his needs. Lord, I know that there is nothing impossible through you. Help me find the answers..... Emmanuel.

ROY

U.S. Army and Caucasian Doctor

Hard knocks is and was all I knew. I had it rough from the start. My parents were military, and therefore that made me military. I could never please my father and my mother just listens in fear of being the next target, he says that I have grown up military and I will leave this house military. So, I tried to prove him wrong and did great in school. I even got an all paid scholarship to Mercer University in Macon, GA to pursue other dreams to be a doctor. One day, my mom and dad said the family was going on a family trip. I didn't know that they were taking me to a military academy to later enlist after I turned of age. I guess it was because things got complicated at home and dad no longer was dad to me. I hated them for that! I went into the Army to be all that I could be and then some on the side. I must admit, they could never catch up with me. Until one day, I decide to let go and admit my blames. Now that I think of it, it was my way out. I never knew the Lord, but my buddy did....I guess a little of me is still with him. I decided to marry a chick, Karen, after doctoral studies and my residency as a medical doctor. All I wanted to do were mixed chemicals.....LOL....I became great at it too. I never look back to visiting or calling my parents and will never forgive them.

KAREN

The Prodigal Daughter

I keep going back and forth on my love for Roy. I decided long ago that I wanted to be comfortable in life. I meet Roy when I was 17 years old and still a minor. I lied and told Roy that I was 18 and a good resource for marriage since I am a trust fund child. My parents wanted to marry me off soon because cancer was slowly deteriorating their bodies and the doctor said they only have 6 to 8 months to live. At any costs, they didn't want me to become a child of the state. My grandparents' inheritance for me wouldn't be granted until I was married. I had no other relatives to rely on. So, they arranged a wedding with Roy, the son of my father's co-buddy, Captain Duke, in the Army. Too bad dad wasn't able to do his research first...He and mom died before I turned 18. Lord, I wish I could have turn back the hands of time.....now that I look back.

UNCLE EARL

The Ex-Convict

God, please grant me the serenity to change the things I can, understand the things I cannot, and the wisdom to know the difference. It has been 30 years since juvenile jail, age 17, and the charged with assault and murder of a prison guard while at Rogers Prison at age 18.

I can remember that day like it was yesterday. Correction Officer Burton ridiculed me in remarks that I would not make it out of prison the same. He says that guys in here haven't seen a young thing in a long while. I immediately punch him in a powerful thrust that my hands shake seeing him fall on some pieces of glass that an on duty female officer was in means to get up. Although I spent years of my life proving him wrong, I cannot forgive myself that I took another man's life.

Officer Burton had two little boys who he never got to play football with. Both boys are now in professional football league. I think back on how now I cannot give my wife, Tangy, the children she wants. Tangy, a Sunday school teacher, and I, a loyal deacon, continues to be dedicated stewards at St. John's Baptist Church despite our perceived misfortunes. We both are able to conceive; however, somehow I feel that this is God's way of punishing me.

In a serene voice, his conscious chants this bible verse, "The Lord is my shepherd; I shall not want. He makes me to lie down in green pastures; he leads me beside the still waters. He restores my soul; he leads me in the paths of righteousness for his name's sake. Yea, though I walk through the valley of the shadow of death, I will fear no evil: for thou art with me; thy rod and thy staff they comfort me. Thou prepare a table before me in the presence of mine enemies: thou anoint my head with oil; my cup run over. Surely goodness and mercy shall follow me all the days of my life; and I will dwell in the house of the Lord forever (Psalm 23:1-6 KJV).

Bryson, my nephew, has also lost his way Lord; he was such a humble person. I guess a bad drinking habit and a father who uses military tactics instead of love can get the best of us. Although I am now mentoring to young troubled men and practicing law in the justice system; Bryson disrespectfully turns a cheek with mentioning how he run his household as a family man.

TANGY

The Virtuous Woman

As I look back in life, I can truly say that GOD favors me. There were times when I didn't do what all I was supposed to do... BUT GOD...always stepped in on time to give me HIS grace and mercy.

I spent most of my adult life trying to find love in all the wrong places. I remember my brother Michael, telling me that I attract the wrong kind of man and that I deserve so much more. Yet, I still tend to settle just to be held. One day while in church service, Pastor Marks was speaking on the subject of love, what it is and what it is not. Ful-filled....yes ....and void.....no.... that was the message. Pastor preached in the Good Book from John 3:16, "For GOD so loved the world that he gave HIS one and only Son, that whoever believes in HIM shall not perish but have eternal life (John 3:16 NIV). He spoke on how GOD's love is beyond limits and that when we seek love; it should be everlasting and he went on talking about the value of being a bridegroom and the rewards for waiting. That day, I became celibate. Michael and his companion, Shawn, would throw a celibacy party every year to celebrate my commitment to myself and GOD along with others we knew. Although my brother has his own issues, he never turned away from reading the Word and knowing Jesus. And then.... And then, comes my Boaz, Xavier Earl Gilmoore.

THE GAY COUPLE
Michael (African-American)

Shawn and I met at The Essence Festival about years ago. We exchange numbers and have been friends ever since. We found a nice condo close to my little sister, Tangy. I still don't believe that she forgives me for not being there physically with her surgery and many break-ups. Poor sister, she attracts "crumb snatchers".....guys who only have their hands out for sex, money, or want you to take care of them. I talk with her every day on the phone though; but, I guess that's not the same as embracing her though it. Before now, I have been selfish, enjoying life and traveling to the next big thing to the next...... from big towns of Detroit and Chicago to countries like France and Spain. Never really felt the need to settle down and be normal. What is normal anyways? I can remember the looks I got at St. John's when I came out but still wanted to be a member. Every fellowship seemed like I could never fit in; so I ran. I ran away from the shame of looking different ..... and I never looked back. Tangy has never forgiven me for leaving. She is the only family I have now. Shawn has been the backbone to my existence. He takes care of me mentally, physically, as well as emotionally. He changed the way I thought of life. Shawn gave me new eyes, that despite us being the attraction of everyone else's insecurities, we can love. With that, I decided to move back to Atlanta only five minutes from my beautiful sister, Tangy and her fiance', Earl.

Shawn (Caucasian)

I came from a GOD-given family. Both my mom and dad raise me in the light of love. They knew from when I was a young boy that I was special.... They call me their "love bug" and the nickname "Bug" stood with me throughout my childhood now into my adult life. I was always gay. I never wanted or desired to be with a woman. But, I did like the way they dressed..... Fierce.... So after high school; I started to dress, walk, and talk more of a woman. I had several jobs, including bank teller, customer service rep, and ....Oh Yeah... flight attendant. But, what I love the most is my job or shall I say career now, Showgirl. Regulars here in Atlanta know me better as.... "Lady Bug."

CHAPTER TWO

The Power of Faith Sermon

The Church is filled with members and friends rejoicing at the sounds of faith and belief as the First Lady testifies on faith and then deliverance. The Holy Spirit touches her with the warmth of forgiveness and servitude.

Suddenly First Lady Kelly shouts with joy as tears run down Pastor Marks' cheeks. Only the two of them knows the history behind this encounter but each individual member begin to feel a peace to whatever problems he or she face when entering the sanctuary that day.

Pastor Marks: (The St. John Baptist Choir Begins to Sing, "I won't Complain" in the background as the pastor begins to speak) "Sometimes we have some rough days and sleepless nights but when we look around and find a light at the end of the tunnel, we found our good days outweighs the bad ones.

GOD has tested the idea of faith from the beginning of time with the tree of knowledge in Genesis Chapter 2:9. The tree of knowledge represents life as being good and tests our faith with evil. The Bible explains how eating from this tree will give knowledge of what's good and evil. It is up to our faith in God to distinguish right from wrong and how to lead a path less followed and of righteousness.

Sometimes when we received too much knowledge we begin to question the Lord and forget that He is GOD. We feel that we can do things when and how we like it without reaping the rewards of disappointment from GOD. GOD says that I am the truth and the life....... (Pastor Marks continues) and without Him the prior we would not have any relevance.

> *Sometimes when we received too much knowledge we begin to question the Lord and forget that He is GOD.*

Shortly after, a young voice starts singing spirit.., spirit..., spirit.... fall down on me. The choir begins to come in and follow the young girl's angelic voice. Pastor Marks makes an alter call and pray for the congregation. Afterwards, the ushers ask the returning of new visitors as he or she walks out of the sanctuary that day, making sure each person feels welcomed to come back to St. John

Baptist Church.

First Lady Kelly: (while meeting Pastor Marks in his study at St. John's Baptist Church) "Hi Marks, we still on for Trudy's (a country buffet)?"

Marks: "Honey, that sounds good! Meet you at the car in ten."

First Lady Kelly: "Ok, Papito[2] (while leaving the church study where Marks and his assistant were locking up)!"

Marks (under his breath): "I love it when she calls me daddy (loving Kelly's Spanglish accent)!"

Marks (thinking about the leftovers in the fridge and how he doesn't have the strength to confront his wife about overeating): "Lord, I really feel I need to talk to her about it, but; I don't want her to think I am failing out of love with her because of her looks as she always plots. I sometimes talk to Minister Jones and he suggested telling Kelly at the right time....but Lord, I just don't know how.

Minister Jones (entering into the study and a little dismayed): "Going to Trudy's again....I have known you and First Lady

---

[2] Daddy

for years now and when the Lord says wait; then, that's what we have to do. Although, we get weary, we cannot give up. First Lady loves you and in the end will follow.

Pastor Marks (smiling favorably): "Lord, you are in control!"

CHAPTER THREE

MEETING THE BROBASKI'S

Roy and I have known each other for years, playing spades every Sunday evening while Karen fried fish for our traditional feast. Karen always teases me about not having a committed relationship, while bending over to put the apple pie in the oven for dessert later. I had felt distant for a long time because of the absence of my first wife. Now, that I have Rachel in my life; I know a change is going to happen in my life. At least, I pray!

"Oh, Baby!" Bryson cried, "Thank you so much for last night! You were amazing! I love you!"

(He leaned over and whispered into my ears.)

"Now that you discovered what I need, our lives are complete," continued Bryson!"

I slowly smiled at him as he kissed me while walking out of St. John Baptist Church. The church welcomed us with our two kids and continued to minister to us on several aspects of life. Bryson and I have been dedicated members for the last past years under Pastor Marks and his wife First Lady Kelly guidance.

Before pulling off in rush to get home, we see a couple approaching us. Bryson and I want to go home to cuddle before picking the kids up from grandma's house. Both of them had to be living in Buckhead, Georgia for a while because of their sense of style and wittiness.

Karen: "Hi, neighbors. Roy and I saw you moving in yesterday. Welcome to the neighborhood."

Rachel: "Oh, I am sorry. It was only I who moved in yesterday. Bryson and I had just gotten married and we decided to take his place."

Roy (with a Colgate smile): "Would you like to come over later for tea with my wife and me?"

Bryson (looking uneasy): "Maybe tonight will not be a good night. But, we will let you know when we are ready ..... (he paused).... to visit!"

I have known Bryson for all my adult life. He would always ask me to join the choir while surprisingly hearing me sing, Loving You, to my unborn, beloved Jeremiah at a nearby park. His father left me to follow his attorney dreams at an upstate law school, and me losing Jeremiah instantly while hearing about his decision to leave us. Since then, all I wanted was stability in my life. So cupid brought me Bryson, a man so chic, fine, and with a plan and a smile that no one could say no to. Cupid puts an arrow in my heart everyday as I listen to his angelic baritone voice in the choir stands at church.

Rachel: "God, could this be real?"

CHAPTER FOUR

HOMELESS

As I lay down on my personal cot, I look out the barred windows of the building for drug addicts and prostitutes. I realize that all I have been running from has hit me head-on like an eighteen wheeler losing control of the wheel. It's funny how GOD works. I knew one day I would have to face my fear; but, I didn't know it would be today. All I can think of is Samantha and Kyle; but know it would be years before I will see them again. I still sneak out while supposed to be grocery shopping or heading for an appointment, authorized personal errands they call it. FBI agent, Sherry Conaway, is my first point of contact.

I cannot believe I'm here, trapped, and without freedom. Most of the time, the toilet do not work, ladies are fussing or fighting, and my personals stay missing. If this is not Hell, I don't want to go there. This means, I will have to adjust and do what I need to....to get to where I want to be. I have a promise apartment and am eligible for an assistance program financially until I get on my feet....if I dot my I's and cross my T's. As I think about it, it all can be worst. Rachel looks down on me when I come by and threatens to call me in. Only if she knew what I know. Then, I hear Sherry coming up the staircase.

Sherry (smiling): "How are you Angie?"

Angie: "Living."

Sherry: "Today, I will have to do another urine test and I have to check your room."

Angie: "Do what you have to do."

Sherry: "Unlike some of the other girls Angie, I really do like you and I know you will meet requirements next appointment for discharge (smiling)."

Angie (while heading to the bathroom): "Looking forward to it! Is all my paperwork transfer to the state department (shouting from the bathroom)?"

Sherry (glad): "Yes, I forward them last week. You will be all set-up for next week appointment."

Angie: "Cool beans (smiling and handing the urine sample to Sherry)."

Sherry (smiling): "I have something I think will help you get to next week."

Angie (confuse): "What is it?"

Sherry: "It's the Holy Bible, the Word of Jesus Christ!"

Angie: "I don't know. I usually don't believe in anything I cannot touch (unsure)?"

Sherry: "Trust me....You can touch Him."

Angie: "Well, okay. Thanks."

Sherry: "Try starting with the book of John. And, if you have any questions or just want to talk my personal number is 478-555-5556 (as FBI agent, Sherry, leaves the building)."

I never thought, I would be without a place I can call home anytime in my life. It felt so good to have my own things and beautiful kids. But, I rejoice that I am without Bryson. Being his wife was like a love story that turned into a horror flick that just wouldn't end. I am thankful I don't have to deal with the expectations of being Mrs. Bryson Dewight Gilmoore. I kind of feel sorry for Rachel though. I guess she will learn for herself. I can truly say that a home is a place where love dwells; and, I will find it on my own......one week and counting. I open my Bible to the start of a new beginning. I turn to the book of John and begin reading, "In the beginning was the Word, and the Word was with GOD, and the Word was GOD..... (John 1:1). Angie continues to read until she came to the end of the book of John. By that time, it was night. She closes the Bible and falls to sleep.

CHAPTER FIVE

IS HE REAL?

For the past years, Michael and Shawn have been there for me...throwing me these celibacy parties were all people we know and friends of people we know come and have a good time. Shawn says comically that this will be a great way for me to meet Mr. Right. I think back to all previous parties (as I prepare for No Milk or Hazlenut in my Coffee Bash, which means no surprises to love.....only the real deal) and laugh at remembering Shawn running down the street in his birthday suit after a friendly dare while playing games.

Tangy (still laughing in private): "Michael, do you think we have

enough decorations?"

Michael: "If not, I will go back to the store when we're done

sis (excited about this year's party and gluing the black,

white flowers to a hanging display over the doors and windows of Tangy's house).

Sometimes, I question GOD about the timing of finding that perfect mate. But then, I remember it's better to wait than to swallow in regrets. GOD's way of doing things; sometimes, don't align with ours. It's just a dry season right now; but, I know it all will come to pass.

Tangy: "How many people have RSVP?"

Shawn (coming from outside putting up clear lights): "Yes, I have the list right here (showing Tangy)."

Tangy (concerned): "One hundred people are going to fill my house?"

Shawn and Michael (harmonizing): "Yes, lil sis!"

Michael: "Remember that we are doing outside as well as inside this year."

Tangy (a little eased): "Okay. Everyone's wearing white or black?"

Shawn: "Yes, I told all guests."

Tangy: "I hope it will be a success and more guests who are wearing black, will be exchanging colors next year suggesting celibacy (smiling at the purpose of GOD behind the party)."

Tangy (smirking): "Hey guys, what color are you all wearing (then laughing)."

Shawn (smiling): "Very funny Tangy! Just because Michael and I haven't gotten married yet doesn't mean we are wearing white (starting to zone out a little)!"

Michael and I have talked about going ahead and making us official; but, Georgia doesn't support gay marriages. For all I have to say, we are married because Michael and I have made a commitment long ago to honor, cherish, and love each other..... and that's enough for me. St. John's is a little different now with the leadership of Pastor Marks and Mrs. Latina Diva, First Lady Kelly. I love to hear her talk. She would always say to us, "Hola tipos! Dado la bienvenida!"[3]

Tangy: "Shawn stop! You just stapled party ribbon to my dinner table!"

Shawn: "Sorry sis....just thinking a little."

Tangy: "Well, come back to planet earth please (smiling)."

---

[3] Hi Guys! Welcomed!

Michael: "Tangy, I have a surprise for you; but, you have to wait 'til tonight (excited)."

Tangy (confused): "Okay big head...no gag gifts this year..... I still haven't gotten over the paint that was made from mud for my facial gift at the last celibacy party...kay?"

Michael (smiling): "Okay (then laughing)."

Michael (thinking ahead): "Sis, what are you wearing?"

Shawn (looking at Michael then Tangy inclusively): "Yea sis.... I think you should wear that off-the-shoulder number with heels."

Tangy (undecided): "I don't know guys.... It may send the wrong impression?"

Shawn and Michael (together): "That's the point!

Michael: "Sis, if you wait any longer; your eggs are going to dry up."

Tangy: "Ha Ha....very funny guys!"

Tangy: "Well, what the heck.... I will wear it because I do look good in it (making sure to point this out)!"

That day went by fairly quick. Tangy, Michael, and Shawn put up all the decorations for the "No Milk or Hazlenut in my Coffee

Bash." Tangy catered the event with seafood dishes and a table full of desserts. Yes, she burns....in a good way!

Michael (still excited): "Sis, this food is on deck!"

Michael (leaving to get ready under his breath): "I know Earl is going to (getting quieter) fit right in."

Tangy: "Did you say something Michael?"

Michael: "No sis, see you in a few."

Shawn (kissing Tangy on the cheek while following Michael): "See you later Tangy!"

As soon as the boys leave, Tangy gets her iPhone and takes a picture of all the decorations and foods she'd made and post it on Facebook. She then turns on Mary J. Blige CD and plays "Just Fine" while dancing to the beat. She closes her bedroom door..... thinking on how put together she will be tonight.

Michael (ringing Tangy's doorbell): "Hi Sis, me and Shawn is at the door (then knocking on the door)."

Tangy (finishing her last touches to her make-up): "Okay.... coming!"

Tangy (opening the door): "Hi guys....right on time (smiling)!"

Shawn (in awl): "Wow, you look great!"

Michael (adding on): "Oh Yeah, I forgot to tell you I invited someone that I think you will find interest in...."

Tangy (a little nervous): "Really, I better change into something more conservative (about to go into her room to change outfits but being stopped)."

Michael (stopping Tangy): "No sis, you are cute and you look available and that's the idea (smiling in admiration)."

Within the next hour, many friends and friends of friends came. All the while, Tangy anticipating which guy would be the guy Michael wanted her to be introduced. Guests complimented Tangy on the food and how her house décor looked for the party. People outside all dressed in either white or black were dancing to a little Charlie Wilson and Robin Thicke along with Teena Marie and Whitney Houston old school. White mostly filled the room with a few specks of guest wearing black. Michael and Shawn wore matching black outfits from the designer, Polo. Tangy's Donna Karen designer white dress set the mood for the occasion....available but committed..... ten years and counting. Many guys approach her; but, none of interest to Tangy. Then, all of a sudden, a gentlemen dressed in all white with a wide-brimmed hat tilted to the side came through the main door of Tangy's house. The ladies all look with admiration; yet, the mysterious gent came right up to Tangy and said....

Xavier Earl (with a big smile): "Hello, you must be Tangy?"

Tangy (a slight pause and exhale): "...... Hi (and then hearing GOD saying ...it's him)."

Xavier Earl: "I'm Xavier Earl. I have heard so much about you from Michael and Shawn."

Tangy (smiling): "I'm Tangy Summers."

Xavier Earl: "That's Gilmoore (and thinking she's the one)."

Tangy: "Well hello Mr. Xavier Earl Gilmoore. Could I get you a drink?"

Xavier Earl: "Yes, pop will do just fine."

Tangy (feeling the chemistry): "Okay, I'll get you a Pepsi."

Michael (approaching): "Hi man, I'm glad you've find the place okay."

Earl: "Yea...GPS took me right here."

Earl (smiling): "Tangy, your sister....one word stunning (still smiling)."

Michael (smiling): "It's genetics!"

Earl: "I guess it skip you and went right to your sister (then laughing)!"

Michael: "Still not funny (not smiling)."

Shawn: "Hey guys….it's time for board games (excited)!"

Games, dancing, eating, fellowshipping, and laughs went on until early the next morning. Soon there was only Xavier Earl, Tangy, Michael, and Shawn left at the well entertained celibacy bash. Shawn drove Michael home because it was very obvious that he had too much wine. Xavier Earl offered to help clean up and Tangy says okay; but, didn't know that this early morning will soon to lead to much more and the end of her ten year draught.

Tangy (refreshed with clothes everywhere): "I guess I will not be
      wearing white at the next celibacy bash?"

Xavier Earl (laughing): "That's makes two of us (then smiling)!"

The two of them never left each other's side. It's funny how GOD works things out! Earl and Tangy knew this wasn't only for one night. In our waiting, we must keep a humble heart and know that GOD is GOD. He doesn't make mistakes. There is no one before Him and there will be no one after Him. He is Alpha and Omega, the beginning and the end. Remember He does hear our cries for help. For the Word says, "I sought the Lord, and He heard my cry and delivered me from all my fears (Psalm 34:4)." At that turning point when both Tangy and Xavier Earl let go of their fears (fears of loneliness, regrets, and past hurts) and trust GOD; He changed those fears to be that of yesterday and blessings of today. Later, they shared a bond that turned into a profound spiritual connection. He is El' Shaddai.

CHAPTER SIX

IS THAT LOVE?

THE BROBASKI'S

Roy and Karen are very loving, spontaneous individuals. Every day I would see Roy give her an arrangement of flowers, each complementing the dresses that she wears and as he glazes into her blue eyes and touches her blonde hair. Looking at The Brobaskis remind me why I enjoy being married to Bryson.

Roy and Karen decided to have their Tuesday Tea. We declined them again as usual and decided to take the twins to the park instead. After leaving the park with Susanne and Kyle, Bryson told me that he has a surprise for me; but, it would not be here until Tuesday.

LOVE LOST

As I took my morning walk on Tuesday before work, my bones in my legs started aching. When this happens usually sometimes bad or unsettling is about to happen in my life. The first time my joints ache, I was begging Bryson to not work so late and to come home to me, his wife. That didn't work, Bryson grunt at me and said, "You know what I need!"

I couldn't have imagined that I was so in love with my husband after all these years and was not enough for him. I had tried my different things to please my husband; but, it was not enough.

I sit down on my office sofa and begin to decide if I wanted my marriage and the twins, Susanne and Kyle, in my life or the thoughts of leaving with nothing. When Bryson and I married, I was barely making ends meet. Grandma Susie and I had difficulties making ends meet while I went to business school; but really, all I wanted to do was sing like Recee. I ended up working the money markets; and I must admit, I am very great at it. The only one who cares now is Grandma Susie.

I had never felt a comfort until I started dating Bryson...He is my one and only! I couldn't see myself starting over again. The air I breathe and the love I know. How can I reject the only person who cares? While texting Bryson a loving acceptance, Angie call again to see the kids.

Angie (thinking how good Bryson is with boundaries): "Hi Rachel, I know we haven't met yet, and; I wanted to know if I can get the Susanne and Kyle this week to go to the zoo?"

Rachel: "I don't think that's possible, Angie. Bryson says that you are not allowed to come 100 feet of the kids and I support him!"

Angie: "Bryson is not the Atlanta police and I will be getting my kids in due season! He will reap what he sows."

Rachel: "Good-bye Angie (while hanging up the telephone)!"

I cannot believe after all this time; Angie still thinks she has the ability to take care of Samantha and Kyle after leaving them on our porch without diapers or food to work in some club as a dancer. Bryson told me how he tried to stop her and said he was taking the twins.

Angie (while hanging up the phone at her two bedroom apartment): "I cannot believe that she is falling for his lies."

Years ago, Bryson and I decided to move and elope to Buckhead, GA from Augusta, GA after finding out that I was pregnant. He never asked me to marry him officially. Bryson's mom, Evelyn, and dad, Troy, did not approved of me since they say I was a "bastard drug baby," as his dad told Bryson in confidence when telling him we were getting married and thinking no one was listening. Bryson loved me despite my drug habit and insecurities, Jean, my mom, introducing me to the fast life after leaving for prison for streetwalking among other charges.

Angie (cutting on the local radio station): "Lord, I know in due season....this too shall pass."

Pastor Marks (broadcasting the Word through the local radio station): "God wants us to depend on Him for everything and every

decision we make... there is a need to confine in Him before acting...
As we say... let me pray about it. When we make decisions without
going to the Father, they fall apart and sometimes change the course
of our lives altogether. Rather deciding to take a job offer, end a
relationship, take a certain route when driving, or even wanting
the impossible, we must take ALL things to God in prayer. Making
decisions and not having God in them, gives Satan the opportunity
to influence our lives negatively. Remember you will reap what you
sow... You may not reap today, tomorrow, or this year....but; in due
season, it will come to pass. If in turn, we sow good seeds by faith,
then there will be a harvest and life purpose will be full-filled. If we
sow bad seeds, there will be no harvest, but a dry or dead patch
in our lives that will need forgiveness and thus healing. Be careful,
but prayful, and allow God to guide your minds and hearts to Him.

THE FIRST NIGHT

I think back on how Angie gave up a good life and a good man. I came home from work excited and anxious about what Bryson has in store for our night. I thought maybe he was going to take me to the play, "Singing Sistas" that I have been bugging him about (smiling)... I hope so. This will make up for all those nights our schedules have been colliding because of either him or me working late...... (Suddenly the phone rang).

Rachel: "Hello, the Gilmoore residence."

Karen (in a high-pitch voice): "Hi Rachel, How are you?"

Rachel: "Fine.... May I ask who is speaking?"

Karen: "This is Karen Brobaski, your neighbor. I am so honored that you and Bryson finally decided to make Roy and I invitation tonight. I am cooking pies and Roy has the tea! I hope you are up for a late night?

Rachel: "Oh Yes (in dismay), Bryson said that he has a special surprise. We will be over as soon as he gets home from his work meeting.

Karen: "Okay, we will be waiting."

Rachel: "Dang, her voice sounds like an electric siren that just won't be quiet unless you unplug it. Maybe, it would not bother me later (questionable).

Rachel (hanging up the phone and under her breath): "I cannot believe Bryson. Well, I guess it's time we meet our neighbors. They seem like really fun people. It could be worse. At least we can spend a night out. Even, if it means company (while walking upstairs to get dress).

Bryson (entering the house around 7 o'clock in the late afternoon): "Hi Sweetie, I'm home!"

Rachel: "Hi darling (calling from upstairs)! Karen Brobaski called (while walking to greet Bryson in a hot pink dress and lipstick to match awaiting for his response).

Bryson: "Wow, you look great! I guess you know we're having tea with Roy and Karen?"

Rachel: "Yes (smiling in admiration)."

Bryson: "I have one question... Are you ready to give me what I need?"

Rachel: "I will always."

As Bryson and Rachel approached the Brobaski's porch, they can smell the pies that Karen mentioned. Bryson grabs Rachel hands and starts rubbing the palms of her hands softly....

Bryson (thinking to himself): "Baby, tonight is going to change your life forever!"

As soon as I walked through the door, I felt my bones ache again. However, this was different than before. It was an excruciating pain that didn't seem it wouldn't go away. Roy answered the door and I feel into his arms.

Roy (surprised): "Bryson, I didn't know she would be this intense about tea! I will give her something to soothe the pain (as he puts me on the sofa in the den).

Karen: "You think she can handle it so soon."

Roy: "I'll make sure it's a minor relaxer."

Roy goes to his pick-me-up bag of candy as he calls it... the ecstasy he was anticipating given Rachel a little later that evening. A blackout cast over Rachel as she forgets the events of last night.

Rachel constipating what happened the night before and a terrifying headache.

I really do not know or cannot remember how a great time Bryson and I had the night before; but, I do remember just morning... Wow, I cannot believe Bryson has it like that! We haven't made love over two months now because of his busy schedule. I would always initiate; but, he usually says he's too tired.... (smiling)... My bones don't ache anymore... Yet, I feel a need for more. I pop another candy (too bad I still didn't know what it was; but knew it made me feel good) out of the bottle that Roy left for me. I cannot wait for another tea if it means that Bryson will forget about being uptight and controlling; and, we can start back the love in our marriage. Lord, guide our hearts and mind to you... For you are Jehovah Jireh. Suddenly, the phone rang...I transfer the call to my cellular because I was running late for work.

First Lady Kelly (chanting Our Father's Prayer):

"Our Father, Who art in heaven

Hallowed be Thy Name;

Thy kingdom come,

Thy will be done,

on earth as it is in heaven.

Give us this day our daily bread,

and forgive us our trespass against us;

and lead us not into temptation,

but deliver us from evil. For thine is the kingdom,

the power, the glory forever. Amen."

(Matthew 6: 9-13)

Rachel (in a hurry): "Hi Mrs. Kelly. Is anything wrong?"

First Lady Kelly: "Rachel, I called you this morning because I was troubled in my spirit last night and I need to give you this information. Come by the church after work tonight. We have a worship service and I need for you to attend.

Rachel: "Okay, Mrs., Kelly. I'll be there (hopping into my BMW sports car)."

CHAPTER NINE

THE WARNING

Pastor Marks (flowing with inspiration and inclusiveness at Wednesday night worship service): "There is nothing new under the sun...what once was will be again. Sin has a history all in itself. God says, ""There hath no temptation taken you but such as is common to man: but God is faithful, who will not suffer you to be tempted above that ye are able; but will with the temptation also make a way to escape, that ye may be able to bear it"" (1 Corinthians 10:13). This world is an imperfect, temporary dwelling place that soon will be destroyed. Rest assured that there is light at the end of the tunnel .... For, external life is yours if only you believe. Say with me (various congregational members and visitors recites in their hearts), "Lord, you are King and Savior...you died on the cross for my sins, and rose to give me everlasting life...I know that you will be coming back for me...my strength and redeemer" This is a world-wide warning. God says that he is coming back for his children. The save shall inherit

the earth and have eternal life but the unsaved will be cast in hell.
Accept Him today and walk in your destiny.

As I think back to Tuesday tea, the blockage that once was there was gone or at least I think. In unbelief, I remember Roy and I together like Bryson and I was this morning. In that moment I saw two visuals in my vision --a light far off and a shade of darkness hovering over me. Maybe that just this new medicine Roy gave me starting to talk (Lol). I know now why Mrs. Kelly asked me to come because the Lord showed her, like always, that trouble was over me and...... because she wanted me to help her with Woman With a Purpose Meeting, ironically (given a slight laugh). Despite my true conscious, I decided to confront Bryson about the events that pondered my mind while at Wednesday night service. It seems at that moment a ball of despair shadowed my stomach and I need some answers. When I got back home, I plotted out exactly what I would say to Bryson; but, nothing would come out right in fear of what may or may not take place. And, plus he looked so happy that I agreed to sharing at Tuesday Tea. I was scared to know if it's true that my husband would condone such behavior, being in the church, a choir director among other discipleships. How could this be? I needed the closure. Will I leave him and have nothing if this is true? How would I manage starting over? I feel like I'm in a terrible horror movie that just won't end (despairing awaiting the truth).

CHAPTER TEN

THE VISIT FROM GRANDMA SUSIE

I can truly say that Grandma Susie is a funny old lady but knows the Bible like tying her shoes. I love my grandma for the patience and understanding she has about Bryson, the twins, I not being able to visit, and not making a fuss when Bryson says its bad timing. As Bryson and I finished breakfast, the cab was outside. And before I could get to the door, the twins were outside hugging Grandma Susie. Grandma Susie was in a bright colored summer dress with cute white sandals that I brought for her. I welcomed her with a warm embrace and yell for Bryson who was in the study.

Grandma Susie (smiling): "Hi daughter! I am so glad to see you it's been almost a year."

Rachel (tears rolling from her eyes): "Hi Mama! So glad to see you...I missed you (giving Grandma Susie a kiss on her cheeks)."

Grandma Susie got settled in the guest room, but couldn't ignore the fact that Rachel seemed a little worried.

Grandma Susie (calling Rachel to her bedroom): "Rachel baby... come here when you finish with the twins (Rachel was reading the twins their favorite fairytale book called, "Little Misfit Singers" in which the twins are read to once a day with Rachel).

Rachel: "Yes Mama (entering the bedroom)."

Grandma Susie: "Rachel is there something you want to talk about. I know Bryson has been uptight lately...I can hear him in the background when we talk on the phone.

Rachel (with sadden eyes): "Actually mom, Bryson is okay now."

Grandma Susie (questionable): "Are you okay."

Rachel (trying to seem like everything okay when looking into Grandma Susie eyes): "Yes."

Grandma Susie: "Alright daughter..... I will leave this subject alone 'til you ready to talk."

Rachel: "Thanks Mama."

Bryson tells Rachel that he is leaving for couple of hours to visit Uncle Earl, while she think about giving him what he needs, and will be back in time for dinner. Bryson pulls up at Uncle Earl home and Tangy, Uncle Earl's fiancé, is there frying fish and making grits. The smell of fried fish brings Bryson back when his dad, Troy, and Uncle Earl would spend all day at a neighborhood pond and fish. Dad catching all the fish and Uncle Earl holding the entertainment by telling jokes and teasing dad. Uncle Earl can be opinionated at times and always have something to say..... it's never a dull moment with my uncle.

Bryson (opening the backyard gate): "Hi Unk and Auntie. How are y'all doing?"

Tangy (smiling at her soon-to-be handsome nephew): "Blessed....
Earl has gotten the promotion as finance head of the
deacon committee at St. John's (K-12) Alternative School
for the older kids along with Sunday school duties every
Sunday. Also, we have great news!

Bryson (looking at Uncle Earl): "Should I sit down for this?"

Uncle Earl: "I can see a limp in your walk and the grey on your
head has a mind of its own.... So... (with a serious face)...
maybe that wouldn't be a bad idea?"

Bryson (smiling): "Ha Ha, you're a hoot Unk but you know I'll get
you back right?"

Uncle Earl (seriously): "Youngster, stay in your lane (broaden up
his shoulders to show off his biceps).

Tangy (excited): "Earl and I have decided to adopt a baby. We
have any interview coming soon with an adoption agency.

Bryson (happily inclined): "I'm excited for you two... It's been a
long time. What made y'all decide to go this route? I believe

that God will send you what you want.... Just don't stop praying."

Uncle Earl: "We are not getting any younger (smiling at Tangy).

Tangy (thinking back on being older and having many doctors telling her that she have bad eggs with only a few left... and the fibroid surgery helped but figured she will not know for sure 'til she have a bundle of love in her wounds): "Don't say that Earl (as she runs into the house while the grease is still popping)!"

Bryson (confused): "Will Auntie be alright?"

Uncle Earl: "Yea, she gets like that sometimes. But, just in case... could you call me later nephew and we can talk. We have a lot of catching up to do since your marriage."

Bryson: "Okay, I will catch you later (getting into his silk black Jaguar)."

Tangy can see the little red robins chirping outside her window. She sighs and prays silently to herself. Tangy thinks back on her past and the mistakes she'd made. The college sweetheart who cheated on her after a three year engagement; her ex-husband who wanted her to take care of him while she foots all the bills; and the doctor who she fell in-love with; but, never call the day after have all catered to Tangy's hurts and regrets. Tangy never understood why she attracts the wrong guys until sitting alone in a hospital bed because of the stresses of life overwhelmed her. She realized something. The only person who was there was the Lord. She couldn't believe that He didn't love and leave her like all other men did in her life. Tangy heard a serene still voice say to her, "Do you know who you are?" Tangy heartbroken said, "No, my family and friends left me here (in anger)!" Michael was nowhere to be found and her muse of a boyfriend left her to deal with the pain on her own. Then, the voice said, "You are my daughter and I won't never leave or forsake you…. I love you when you were in your mother's womb…And child, I don't make any mistakes." Tears rolled down Tangy's face in joy. At that moment, Tangy began her recovery in the hospital but all wasn't lost; her relationship with GOD grew stronger every day. Suddenly Tangy's daymare ends as she hears Earl walking through the door.

Earl: "Honey, is it anything I can do to make you feel better?"

Tangy: "Baby, just knowing that you care and is here with me makes things fine. I am glad I am about to be Mrs. Xavier Earl Gilmoore. A girl couldn't pick a better man (kissing Earl on the cheeks).

Earl: "I know (patting Tangy on her bottom)! The fish is ready (thinking about eating)."

Tangy: "I'm ready also (and then the lights in Uncle Earl and Tangy's happily home went out)!"

CHAPTER ELEVEN

THE WEDDING

Earl's family, including Bryson and Rachel, wanted him and Tangy to have a big wedding. But, what the two love birds wanted really was to do their union in Hawaii. So, Earl surprised Tangy early that morning.

Earl (excited): "Tangy sweetheart, Guess what we are doing today?"

Tangy (irritated): "Stop Earl, I'm trying to get the rest of my beauty sleep (mumbling)!"

Earl (still excited): "I think you really want to see what I have … darling!"

Tangy (turning over): "I'm too tired honey ….will rock your world around eleven o'clock….. Kay?"

Earl (cutting on the television and putting in a DVD): "I knew it would be hard to wake you (thinking it is always hard to wake Tangy in the mornings) ....so listen Honey!"

The television DVD: "Aloha.....stressed, overwhelmed about your wedding location. Well, why not get some breeze and sun in Honolulu, Hawaii. We have the best intimate wedding packages. What are you waiting for? It's you time now! So, make it special with us."

Tangy (shouting): "We're going to Hawaii? We're going to Hawaii?"

Earl (shouting with Tangy): "We're going to Hawaii!"

Earl: "How fast can you pack baby?"

Tangy jumped out of bed; dashed across Xavier Earl and grabbed a kiss along the way. Tangy started the shower; holler for Earl to start packing their clothes; and begin singing "Umm Good" by Smokie Norful while in her ten minute early morning shower. Tangy gets out of the bathroom and comes to her vanity mirror to apply her make-up and slips on her favorite pink-flowery dress with a wide-brimmed summer hat made just for Hawaii.

Earl: "Honey, do you think we should leave a note just in-case someone stops by....maybe Michael or Bryson?"

Tangy: "Earl honey, you know phones work in Hawaii."

Earl: "I guess you're right (still excited and thinking about their honeymoon after the ceremony and not getting enough from the night before)."

Tangy is my kind of woman. She is humble and sweet in public; but a cheetah at night. I packed all the love toys, and the ice, candy, and cool whip is already ordered for tomorrow night. Yes, GOD has truly favored me. Look at her as she walks and smiles, I see GOD's grace. I never thought in years I would find a P. Y. T. (as Tangy walks towards Xavier Earl to get into his 2015 white GMC Denali that he finished detailing the day before).

When Xavier Earl and Tangy got to the airport, they felt like packed sardines. Passengers were trying to get to one destination to the next. Yes, it is summer time and travelers are going on vacations. I'm afraid of flights; but, this is the fastest way to get to Hawaii and make our wedding date. It was time.... time to abroad the plane. All of a sudden, I got nauseated. Tangy asks was I okay flying; but, I wanted to go all the way out so we had first class everything: seats, service, food, and wine. I kind of went to an ease when we settled into our private seats. Tangy smile filled the entire plane, like the morning sunshine peaking over the ocean front. Man, I cannot wait to get there.

Tangy (still smiling): "Xavier honey (as she calls when they are in romantic mode)?"

Xavier Earl (a little nervous): "Yes, my right now and future?"

Tangy: "You are holding my hand a little tight."

Xavier Earl (still nervous): "Really, I didn't notice (still clasping her embrace)."

Tangy: "Tomorrow, we will be husband and wife. This moment is one that I have longed for (starting to daydream)."

The Delta plane begins to rumble, the wind and rain outside the plane begin to mash against each other. Xavier Earl started singing "Jesus on the Mainline... I'm going to tell HIM what I want, Jesus on the Mainline....I'm going to tell HIM what I want..... and then he starts again.

Tangy (holding on to Xavier Earl): "Lord, I know Earl can be corny sometimes....but yes Lord, You are the mainline and we ask for your help! ....Help!

Flight Attendant (in a hurried voice): "Attention, we are in a rough area at the moment; but, rest assured everything is under control. Look like we will have a rough landing for our next stop in Honolulu, Hawaii. Please use your belts and air masks for your safety."

The pilot begins to prepare the plane for landing. Carry-on bags and other items, such as headphones, cell-phones, wine and champagne glasses filled begin to fall over. Then, all of a sudden everything stopped and the pilot landed private Flight 202 Atlanta to Hawaii in mint condition. God is good! As the soon to be Gilmoores step onto the sands of the beach that led to their bridal suite, Xavier Earl planted a big kiss upon Tangy's lips. She gently rubbed the excess pink Cover girl lipstick from Xavier Earl's filled-in mustache.

The next day was beautiful! Hawaii customs and staff has traditional flowers, lays around their necks, candles throughout the beach wedding location, and a dessert bar as well as tables full of Hawaiian dishes. Tangy came down the sanded aisle covered with roses. She wears a white flowing princess cut dress with red, pink accents and crystal studs. This was all in the wedding package for hers as a keepsake. Xavier Earl was deck out in a Ralph Lauren designer cut white suit with a red handkerchief to match. The couple decided to go bare-footed just for the occasion. The complimentary finger foods and desserts hit the spot. The couple walked in awl to their bridal suite. Throwing Tangy on the red-rose master bed, Xavier Earl clapped his hands twice to turn down the lights while also tuning the sound response music speakers to play Guy song "Piece of my Love" filled the suite. Xavier Earl and Tangy made love that night. The next day everything was broken all but Earl and Tangy's undefiled love, including the headboard, candles on the tables, and the ceiling fans from Xavier Earl hang-gliding.

CHAPTER TWELVE

THE MARKS

I been married to Marks for years now and cannot believe that I haven't told him why I have been so distant. Ever since I was a little girl, I was told that I would marry in the church and have the American Dream of two and a half kids. I got to admit, I do have the white picket fenced house, the man of my dreams, and it's just a plus that he is a man of God. Along the way, I tainted my chances to have kids with the decision to have an abortion in my early twenties because of dreams of college and not being married. My mom thought that was the best solution to the problem since her good name was at stake in the usher committee at St. John's Baptist Church. Dad was on the deacon committee, but wanted "his grand" as he called the bundle of joy in my stomach. It broke his heart. They are deceased now but somehow I can still hear mom's dictating voice saying, you don't want to mess up our family's good name, The Monroe's. So, I had it…..an abortion that damaged more than my womb, but also my heart. Tears start running down my eyes. I loved him. He was my high school sweetheart and my best friend. I never told him that I was pregnant. I wonder where in life he is now and what could have been. Marks were just like him in the beginning of our marriage. He gave me flowers every Monday with a letter telling me how he appreciate me, and would be very cute when he compliment how I dressed and look. Now, our conversations are centered on church business. I think Marks have given up on the topic kids, but I haven't. There's still a void in my heart. Maybe one day, God would send us the child He has for us. Every time I think back on how painful it is to tell Marks after all these years the real reason, I can't…. I indulged in my favorite, the refrigerator.

Lord, you said that you will give me the desires of my heart. You said that the thoughts You have for me is of good and not evil, to give me a future and a hope when I go and pray to You and I will find You when I pray with all my heart. *(Jeremiah 29:11-13)* Last week, I did made a step to move forward with my deliverance. I joined Weight Watchers, my new alibi. God is still good!

Pastor Marks: "Kelly, do you remember where I save next Sunday's sermon notes. I cannot find them anywhere?"

First Lady Kelly (in Spanglish): "Marks, you never typed it up miel[4]. Sus notas son debajo la carpeta azul[5] .....on your office desk (packing her workout clothes in hopes Marks do not come in their bedroom) Papito.

Pastor Marks (wondering what his wife is doing): "Okay, I've found it (thinking she is probably eating the last piece of pecan pie)!"

First Lady Kelly (feeling refreshed and joyous): "Marks, I will be back a little later. I have an errand to run."

Marks: "Okay (typing and then reading his Sunday sermon)."

Message: Faithfulness
"Good and faithful servants you have been faithful with a few and I will make you ruler of many... The Lord knows all our needs and

---

[4] honey

[5] your notes are under the blue folder

wants...He knows our doubts and fears. We praise Him in advance and when we are going through. God will not let anything come in our lives beyond what we are able to escape or bare. For, He is a perfect, omnipresent, omniscient God.... Who sees all things, knows all things, and loves all things...God is Savior and King! Praise Him now.... For there is "perfection" awaiting in the heavens above. An illustration in the good book of Ruth says, "Now it came to pass in the days when the judges ruled, that there was a famine in Bethlehemjudah went to sojorn in the country of Moab, he, and his wife, and his two sons. And the name of the man was Elimelech.... (Ruth 1:1-2). Ruth, a faithful Moabitess, loved her mother-in-law, Naomi, so much that she stayed faithful to her family and lifetime heritage that Naomi valued. When Naomi gets weary in faith that was claimed hers and asked Ruth and her other daughter-in-law, Oprah, to leave; GOD steps in. GOD allows Ruth's faithfulness to prevail. In her faith to stand by Naomi, GOD blesses the family with another heritage through Elimelech (Naomi husband), Ruth's Boaz.

Marks finished typing the last words of the message as given. Then, he hears God whisper to him "look to your wife." He repeats, "look to my wife" and then shuts down his office computer. Meanwhile, First Lady Kelly turns up her favorite song, "In the Middle" by Isaac Carree. She spins her 2015 candy apple red Cadillac on two wheels in the parking lot of the building for her Weight Watchers support group meeting. Then, she thought to herself, I'm ready Lord!

Faithfulness Sermon Continues (Pastor Marks reading before turning off computer)

"Sometimes, we are so caught up in the now situation that we forget what we prayed and ask God for. We get weary and dismayed in the waiting process that while we are in that "waiting room"…. we forget to keep praying and believing by faith that this too will come to pass."

First Lady Kelly (under her breath): "Oh Yeah, I forgot to call Rachel to see if she started on the itinerary for Woman with a Purpose Meeting (while dialing on her flip phone in determination to never upgrade because she feels that the flip phone is vintage and …. Oh Yass…stylish)."

CHAPTER THIRTEEN

DR. Z TALK SHOW

Rachel (as the phone rings): "I'll just let the answering machine pickup.... Bryson says this is our night (thinking about having adult time with The Brobaski's and watching DOC Z, a talk show).

Lord, is it wrong for me to want to satisfy my husband. I cannot see myself without him. He is my song and dance. I can't lose Bryson Gilmoore. He is the only man; who was there for me, understood, and care for me when that rippling pain from my past settled in my bones. Everyone does this and I ain't any different! ......What do DOC Z knows? He is not married and the divorce was so quick, I almost forgot his wife's name. These days it's hard to find a good man because of arrest records, the other man next door, and not to mention the lies. I know there are good men out there.... somewhere..... The church doesn't have to know...... or do they?

Television Dialog

Woman Guest on Show: "I been swinging for years now with my husband and wouldn't change a thing. He is happy; therefore, I am happy!"

DOC. Z: "Swinging is a new world idea that came about because married couples have engaged boredom and routine into their marriages. Instead of doing fun, exciting things together; he or she looks outside when they should be looking inside. Swinging allows another woman or man to defile the sanctity of marriage. Couples who are swinging need to regroup before considering this new worldly idea and think of the consequences."

Rachel (after cutting off the TV): "Lord, just this once. I am doing this for my marriage (in an unsure voice).

MY SECOND AFFAIR

It was eleven o'clock and it was completely dark in our master bedroom. Bryson and I have just rolled over from being sleep and the alarm clock begins to ring. My husband lean over and whispered into my ear that he was ready to go over to the neighbor's for tea. It wasn't too fortunate at first, the idea of allowing another woman to feel the comfort Bryson's embrace. I kept telling myself that it is for only one night then things will change.

We arrived with our negligee and silk pajamas on under our clothes. Soon after the normal three knocks on the door, Roy answers the door with a warming smile on his face. The tea was brewing in the kitchen while both the twins were with Grandma Susie...We arrange to have them to stay. I smiled back at Roy as he slowly unbuttons my blouse in interest to Karen who was watching in the kitchen.

Karen (peeping in den): "Anyone up for some hot tea?"

Bryson replies in an intriguing voice: "As long as it's hot and not cold."

Four hours later I wake up in my holified bed of denial and kiss my husband as I take the normal two mile walk that seems to make me feel better. The day after, my bones again ache but this time in a longer duration. When passing by the Brokaski's home who live across the street, First Lady Kelly shouts while trying to get my attention to stop to converse with her the new plans for "Women's with a purpose meeting."

First Lady Kelly: "Rachel, Rachel!" and continues, "Nina[6], you know you hear me." (shouting Latina in a convincing voice).

Rachel: "Hi, First Lady. I haven't yet got the information you need ..... It's been a busy week for me."

---

[6] Girl

First Lady Kelly (cutting her eyes at me): "I will be seeing you at church El domingo[7]?"

Rachel: "I wouldn't miss it for the world!"

---

[7] On Sunday

ℭHAPTER FIFTEEN

A CRY FOR FORGIVENESS

Bryson and I have been swinging for almost one year now along with our first encounter and it still feel fresh and new, but the guilt is decaying my body. I can remember when it first started and the thoughts of my newlywed husband asking me did I change my mind of what I promised him. I was confused at first of what he was asking until the night he took me over to introduce me to the Brobaski's.

Bryson has lived in the neighborhood years before with his first wife, Angie. Angie and Bryson never could get along because she never wanted children; but, a life of partying and late nights. With Susanne and Kyle wanting to be with their mother and Bryson refusing because Angie's drug habit and nightlife. Bryson says he feels that she will never change, although, she has been clean for several years. Bryson has very vague memories of

Angie leaving after an argument and the police escorting her off the premises. Bryson suggests that we do not discuss her.

With all the lies and betrayal of Bryson doing nights by himself with Karen and telling me it's only for that night. I couldn't leave with the countless pounding of his fists hitting me in my face every time if I try in refusal. I even remember the night I had to be taken to the emergency room convincing the doctor that I had fell .....And then, I cried out!

CHAPTER SIXTEEN

THE VISIT FROM ANGIE

The doorbell rand and surprisingly it was Angie. I cannot believe she is here with the restraining order still valid. However, calmness came over me. I needed answers. Did Bryson and Angie have the same problems? Could she enlighten me how she got out of this madness? I opened the door.

Angie: "Morning Rachel, it been a long time (and then noticing that Rachel was in confusion and then the mark on her face that was covered with cosmetics)."

Rachel: "Hi Angie."

Angie: "I got the court order removed and I have to talk to Bryson about visitation."

Rachel: "If you don't mind Angie, I rather you tell him yourself. He will be home later today."

Angie: "Rachel, there is something I need to tell you... Bryson is not a good man. He has a lot of dark secrets and it looks like you know one of them (touching Rachel's make-up and the helm of her smile)."

Rachel: "Could you tell me more (tears running down her cheeks)? I want out."

Angie: "I know Bryson told you that I was the problem in our relationship. But, that's not the entire story. When I first met Bryson, he had it together.....the smile, the flattery, and the love-making. I couldn't get enough of Mr. Bryson Dewight Gilmoore. I was in a bad situation with my mother and her random guy friends. I needed to get out! So, that's what I did....but I ended up in the lion's mouth ready to devour all I am and all I know. Bryson told me if I didn't complete him and his needs he will force me back to the life that my mother is now in jail for. I started telling myself that it was nothing, but then, I got hooked on the Tuesday teas and also the sweet taste of the candies Roy always had laid out for me. After sometime, I realized this wasn't what I wanted so, I packed up Samantha and Kyle and left. Roy has some connections including the police. When I thought I was safe in a hotel room in Tennessee with the kids, I heard a knock of the door. It was the local police. Bryson was with the cops and took my babies from me. I made a mistake and took a candy before laying the kids down for sleep. It showed up in the urine test that Tennessee police gave to me at the station. It all added up when a state counselor, Miss Sherry Conaway, talked to me that night while in handcuffs among drug charges and attempted kidnapping. She stated all the allegations that Bryson committed to and then my eyes lighten up when she told me that she don't work for him, but she would like to help me. Miss Conaway got my sentences dismissed if I agreed to stay in a half-way house and give Bryson full custody of the kids. Rachel, that day was the hardest day of my life. Despite what Bryson told you ... I love my kids and life without them has been void. I struggle for some time with my drug addiction and you know how Bryson reacts when I attempt to see the twins. Because of Miss Conaway, I was able to get off drugs, find me a house and home, a job I love, and the opportunity to rebuild my life totally. This is a summons by the courts to reopen the custody case in hopes of Samantha and Kyle coming home with me. And Rachel, if you need to get away; I live at 202 St. Andrew's Court near Marietta.

Rachel (looking unsure with a humbled voice): "Thank you."

I LOVE YOU

Bryson and I have been seeing our neighbors for a while now and I am tired of letting my soul go down in the pits. I remember my father telling me that I am a ruby filled with uniqueness and clarity pure from the heart and this I should always remember..... and that my merchandise is good.... Dad would read to me Proverbs 31:

"Who can find a virtuous woman? For her price is far above rubies. The heart of her husband doth safely trust in her, so that he shall have no need of spoil. She will do him good and not evil all the days of her life. .....She perceiveth that her merchandise is good: her candle goeth not out by night.....She stretched out her hand to the poor; yea, she reacheth forth her hands to the needy. She is not afraid of the snow for her household are clothed with scarlet. .... She openeth her mouth with wisdom; and in her tongue is the law of kindness.....Her children arise up, and call her blessed; her husband also, and he praiseth her.....Many daughters have done virtuously, but thou excellest them all. Favour is deceitful, and beauty is vain: but a woman that feareth the Lord, she shall be praised" (Proverbs 31: 10-12, 18, 20-21, 26,28-30 KJV).

My father died when I was a teenager and I still carry his spirit with me in all I do. My heart has been broken for years now with Bryson pounding on my heart with his fists, ridiculing my insecurities, and regretting that I was not more like his first wife, Angie.

It seems like my loved husband has begun to show another side that I did not know exists. Rachel begins to sing "Superwoman" by Karen White while still in deep thought and then thinking.... When I cook breakfast, he doesn't have time to eat. And, when I ask to meet for dinner; he has other evening plans. He says that someone needs to work to be able to feed my food habits. I don't know what has come over me, but all I want to do is eat and pray. Yes, I have notice that my weight has picked up lately; but, Bryson do not want me to run or leave the house as much as before. So, to stay safe, the twins and I do things inside.

Singing use to be a profound passion of mine; now, it seems like the music in my heart has found its way dormant deep inside. My recording studio in the downstairs den is now use for Bryson private space for exercising and other activities I do not feel like speaking on at this time.

Finally, I can say that I am where I need to be. How can one know when she is fully redeemed? I've learnt it is when you love GOD with all your heart and mind... For, this is the greatest commandment. I've found peace in my spirit. Although Bryson is still having late nights and still pounds on my face, I know it only was The Lord whom pulled me out of my mess and saved me. Yes, I will always be loved because I know that HE loved me first. I attend church, worship services, and fellowship with the women of St. John's often either when Bryson's gone or at work. Bryson stopped going. Mrs. Kelly Monroe-Marks has been a shoulder to lean on and a friend. Yet, I don't know how to get from Bryson's tight embrace, GOD, has already said to me that this too will pass. I told First Lady Kelly and she gave me this scripture:

"Charity suffereth long, and is kind; charity envieth not: charity vanuteth not itself, is not puffed up, Doth not behave itself unseemly, seeketh not her own, is not easily provoked, thinketh no evil; Rejoiceth not in iniquity, but rejoiceth in the truth; Beareth all things, believeth all things, hopeth all things, endureth all things. Charity never faitheth.... When I was a child, I spake as a child, I understood as a child, I thought as a child: but when I became a man, I put away childish things.......And now abideth faith, hope, charity, these three; but the greatest of these is charity (1 Corinthians 13: 4-8, 11, 13 KJV). LOVE, Kelly.

CHURCH

Pastor Marks (summarizing today's sermon): "Today, we will stand in deliverance from fear of failure. The enemy wants us to tell ourselves that we cannot do something and that we are too far deep in to come out. However, Today is a new day and Lucifer will always be a liar—today, tomorrow, and all the days to come. We endured for a night but joy comes in the morning!"

(The entire St. John congregation stands in reverence of knowing that there is a blessing behind not giving in or up). Pastor Marks continues to preach what fear does to the mind and the soul and the only way to come out is to face it. Every member and friend leaves the church with peace in their hearts, including Rachel.

Pastor Marks: "Fear is an idea that controls the inner self and the decisions which we make. The only way to mitigate a fear concept is the face it head on. That means praying, fasting, and fellowshipping until our prayers have been answered.

Rachel (persuading Bryson to attend that Sunday): "That was an enlightment to my heart!" (I told Bryson as we walked out of church that Sunday evening). Bryson remember that there is nothing too hard for GOD.

Bryson: "Yes, it was (unaware of the implementation of change GOD has implanted and smiling as we walked toward Trudy's)!"

Bryson was thinking in ego of self; the idea that he will once in for all get rid of Angie with the court hearing in a couple of weeks. Bryson is confident that his lifestyle will not change. Rachel is at a turning point in her walk with fear. She starts planning for her future without Bryson. Somehow Bryson has stopped asking Rachel to Tuesday Tea and she doesn't feel the need to ask why. She knows that GOD is working it all for her good. For, she read a bible passage last night that says:

"And we know that all things work together for good to them that love GOD, to them who are called according to his purpose (Romans 8:28)."[8]

Rachel tucks Kyle and Samantha in their beds after reading, "Little Misunderstood." Afterwards, she walks into her bathroom realizing Bryson isn't home yet. Rachel took out the pregnancy test she took months ago that shown two dark red lines in her bottom drawer place in a disguised perfume box with the price tag still attached. Is this Bryson's love child? But, Rachel still not knowing what to do......yet knowing one thing.....she's not going to tell Bryson and thinking only if he knew.

Early when the sun peaks over the darken sky; Rachel decides to get up and pray. She begins by thanking GOD for what HE has already done in her life and what HE is going to do in her life. Rachel looks again at the pregnancy test and then closes her bathroom door. As the sun get brighter and the morning dew begins to subsides, she smiles with joy that there will be a love child. The bundle of love in her stomach will mend the aching facets of her life. Then, the doorbell rings as Rachel opens her white pearl iron door.

Atlanta Policeman: "Hi, is this Mrs. Bryson Gilmoore?"

Rachel (concerned): "Yes, may I help you?"

Atlanta Policeman: "Mrs. Gilmoore, your husband has been arrested and he wanted me to inform you."

Rachel (shocked and unease): "Arrested?"

Atlanta Policeman: "Yes, he is a suspect for attempted murder. We need for you to come to the local police department for a statement."

Rachel (still in disbelief): "Okay, I will be down in a few hours. I need to find a sitter?"

Atlanta Policeman: "That's fine Ma'am."

As I walked down the halls of the police department, several questions pondered my mind. Who was harm? Why is Bryson under investigation? What happened? And, should I be there for Bryson or use this as an excuse to leave? Finally, I came to the specified room that I would do my statement. The officer asked was I aware that my husband stage a fire last night at 202 St. Andrew's Court. My heart started to pound and my bones begin to ache. I told him no. He asked me did my husband have any motives to harm Ms. Angela Lorazdos-Gilmoore. I told the officer that I would like to speak to my husband. The police officer said that couldn't happen because of the allegations brought by Ms. Lorazdos and the fact that Bryson doesn't want to see anyone. But, the officer does contests that Bryson admit to charges and then places an envelope addressed to me in my left hand because my other hand was occupied holding tissues from my flowing tears. As I left the police station that day, I notice the flowers being brighter, the air smelling fresher, and my burdens being lighter. Lord, is it wrong for me to feel this way, my husband may go to prison (as Rachel turned on her car radio)? I must find Angie. Police says that she skip town after making her statements. They don't know her whereabouts legally because Angie is under Miss Sherri Conaway's, FBI agent, care. When I got home the kids were gone and there was a note on the table from Angie (so nervous I knocked over the phone), it said:

Dear Rachel,

"The Lord is my shepherd; I shall not want. HE maketh me to lie down in green pastures: HE leadeth me beside the still waters. HE restoreth my soul: HE leadeth me in the paths of righteousness for HIS name's sake. Yea, though I walk through the valley of the shadow of death, I will fear no evil: for thou art with me; thy rod and thy staff they comfort me. Thou prepares a table before me in the presence of mine enemies: thou anointest my head with oil; my cup runneth over. Surely goodness and mercy shall follow me all the days of my life: and I will dwell in the house of The Lord for ever" (Psalm 23: 1-6 KJV). Samantha and Kyle are with me now. I will contact you at a later date. Angie

Angie

THE FIGHT

My baby Rachel is all I have as I think back. We have been two peas in a pod since my daughter went home to glory. But now, the phone calls seem to get fewer and fewer. It has been a year now and she called once, but then, hurried off the phone as I heard a rumble in the background. I try not to get into Bryson's and Rachel's business; but, he has change. I am not allowed to come to the house only if it's to sit with the twins. My goodness, Samantha and Kyle are almost teenagers. I always send birthday presents; but, that's not the same. I rather see them every day if I can. Lord, look here (as she sees the voicemail light flashes on her landline phone as she stopped rocking in her favorite chair)!

The Answering Machine: "Mama Susie, this is Bryson. I tried
    reaching Rachel, but the phone is busy. I guess you already
    know that I was arrested because of my baby mama and

her drama. Could you tell Rachel that I will be home tomorrow? I got a break, but I still have to go to trial. Love you Mama, Bryson.

Grandma Susie (while calling Rachel on her cellular): "Hi Rachel, are you okay?"

Rachel (while on the phone): "Hi Mama! What a pleasant surprise!"

Grandma Susie: "Talk to me child?"

Rachel: "Mama, I don't know where to start. I thought that maybe I could handle my marriage on my own."

Grandma Susie: "Everyone needs somebody and you aren't any different. If GOD wanted us to be alone, HE wouldn't have made Eve for Adam and since Bryson is not being the man he needs to be, you have me."

Rachel: "You know what Mama..... I am happy you'd said that..... I love you! .... I know you have been interceding and it's been working for me.

Grandma Susie: "Go on child...."

Rachel: "Mama when I first met Bryson, life was good. And then, he begins to change. First the controlling.... in everything I did or don't do. Somehow, I let this slide because I thought

I was doing something wrong and we just started our marriage. We meet the neighbors next door and he...."

Grandma Susie: "Go on child..."

Rachel (hesitating): "Bryson asked me to full-fill his needs by allowing another man and woman into our bed. Mama, I don't want you to think....."

Grandma Susie (praying): "Lord, give me strength. For, You are an omnipresent, omniscient GOD....YOU know all things and YOU are with us always. Lord, I ask in your favor to heal my Rachel's insecurities. Take away anything unclean and that's not like you. Give her strength and wisdom... Oh Lord....to move forward in her life.... And, remove anyone or anything that blocks this blessing that is already done. Amen. Hallelujah. Praise him child.

Rachel (in tears of strength and hope): "Thank you Jesus, Thank you Jesus!"

Rachel (after praising the Lord): "Mama, I knew you had prayed this prayer for me before now because I know you and that's what I was about to say. I looked next door and haven't seen anyone for days. Just morning, I saw a for sale sign on The Brobaski's home. So, I know Bryson will change."

Grandma Susie (puzzled): "I don't know child. But, he did call me on my voicemail and said he will be home tomorrow."

Rachel: "Okay."

Grandma Susie: "Bryson also says that he is in jail? Child what's going on?"

Rachel: "It has something to do with his ex-wife, Angie."

Grandma Susie: "Is the kids alright?"

Rachel: "Yes, but she has them now. Somehow, I have to tell Bryson. I don't know how he will react with knowing his trial will be soon."

Grandma Susie: "Rachel, my concern is you. Do you need me to come over?"

Rachel: "No Mama, I will stop by home when it's a good time. Bye Mama. Love you (anxious about tomorrow)!"

Grandma Susie: "Okay Baby, and remember you can always come home. I love you (hanging up the phone)!"

Rachel (her cellphone begin to ring again): "Hello, This is Rachel Gilmoore?"

Uncle Earl: "This is Earl.... Rachel."

Rachel (smiling): "It's always a pleasure to hear from you Unk!"

Uncle Earl: "I just bailed Bryson out of jail. They will release him tonight."

Rachel: "Tonight?"

Uncle Earl: "Yes, that fool should've paid his alimony. He is so careless. Next time, I am keeping his well-groomed butt in jail.... It will teach him how to be tough (angry because he had to bail him out under Tangy and his financial strain).

Rachel: "How's Tangy?"

Uncle Earl: "She has been under the weather lately, but she goes to see a doctor tomorrow."

Rachel: "I hope all is well. Good-bye Unk. Bryson will be here in a little."

Uncle Earl: "Bye niece (hanging up)."

Lord, YOU are my cornerstone to which I am built. YOU are the map to any situation. YOU are a problem solver. It is impossible to not hear YOU because YOU gave me the key... The Holy Bible.... That rests with me. Give me strength in times of trouble. Rachel opened her Bible to pray for her Auntie Tangy; but, not knowing this pray was for her as well:

"Therefore being justified by faith, we have peace with GOD through our Lord Jesus Christ. By whom also we have access by faith into this grace wherein we stand, and rejoice in hope of the glory of GOD. And not only so, but we glory in tribulations also: knowing that tribulation worketh patience; And patience, experience; and experience, hope: And hope maketh not ashamed; because the love of GOD is shed abroad in our hearts by the Holy Ghost which is given unto us (Romans 5:1-5).

At that moment, Rachel heard a serene voice say, it's time to fight. Right then Bryson comes through the door. Immediately, he calls for Kyle and Samantha, but no answer. He shouts, Rachel! Rachel comes to his call in despair, but with strength in GOD. Rachel repeats, Lord, I know it's time to fight. Bryson takes Rachel by the hair and drags her up the stairs while she feels each bump of each step. Rachel quickly snatches his tight embrace from her hair and runs down the stairs. Rachel remembers the tranquilizers that she left in the drawer from Bryson's drug stash in her old, remodeled studio room. Rachel found them along with other prescription as well as some street drugs. She also discovered the labeled "candies" on a bottle that said Dr. Roy Brobaski. I grabbed the tranquilizer needle and planted it into Bryson's right shoulder as his arm reached for me. Bryson knocked out in less than five seconds from not being able to move his arm to then, thus unmovable.

Quickly, I call the cops to come pick Bryson up. I was ready.... ready to confess and walk forward. I guess Bryson will find out later that the twins are with Angie, but I rested that; he is no longer able to hurt me. I packed up my things and moved back home with Mama. I listen to "Say a Prayer" by Donald Lawrence featuring Faith Evans on my car radio as I praise GOD in amid of it all.

Grandma Susie (opening the door): "Thank GOD, you're home child... you're home (then noticing Rachel on the floor in pain holding herself)!"

Grandma Susie rushes Rachel to the hospital. Rachel's pain has grown into a beautiful baby girl with curly dark reddish-brown hair, blue eyes, and a smile that would win any baby pageant. Although the delivery went great, Rachel's little girl is pre-mature and will need to be in the hospital for a least a year as the doctor explains. Rachel visits Joy Denita Gilmoore, her bundle of love, daily...... yet still had not told Bryson.

CHAPTER TWENTY

AN UNEXPECTED SURPRISE

Tangy remembers the times her and Earl was time after time with doctor after doctor trying to become pregnant and the last physician telling Tangy that it just not possible. After not hearing from the adoption agency that a child was available; Tangy begin to become weaker and weaker in health. She vomited everyday with pains in her abdomen until Earl told her that he is taking her to a medical doctor. Tangy begin to go in and out of sleep while at the doctor's office. In her unconsciousness, she could hear a voice that said:

Doctor Indie Temples (Tangy's religious OB-GYN): "These days one has to be strong in every aspect of their lives. In times of weaknesses.....this is when the devil try to convince us that we are complacent and will not survive our storms. Yet, if we look high into the hills, we will see GOD.....Our Strength,

Redeemer, Guide, Shield, and Buckler. For, HE knows our strengths and weaknesses. And, HE is still there. When the devil say be depressed, stop trying to succeed, you don't matter and then test your faith by saying you will never get what you prayed for. But then, GOD breathes faith in you and says…. Wake Up….you are loved, you are my child, your breakthrough is around the corner, you are beautiful, you will succeed because you have ME guiding and directing your paths….Wake Up…..My child….. You still have work to do. Wake Up Rachel…you are pregnant!"

Rachel (slowly speaking): "Pregnant?"

Doctor Indie Temples (glad to say again): "Yes, Rachel. We thought it was not possible; but, you are!"

Uncle Earl (shouting at the top of his lungs): "Yes, Yes…. we're pregnant (hugging and kissing Rachel)!"

C HAPTER TWENTY-ONE

I DIDN'T KNOW.

Something about this day seemed different. Shawn didn't beat me to the kitchen to get the last bowl of oatmeal. He didn't pull the covers off of me to wake me up. He was just lied there—sleeping. I got up and fixed us both a bowl of oatmeal and bananas with coffee and vanilla creamer. I figured he was tired from work late last night at the club. I have gone to the club a couple of times to see him perform as "Lady Bug." The crowd loves him; always throwing flowers and money at his feet as he serenades them with oldies. I went back to our bedroom and Shawn started to speak.

Shawn (concerned): "Michael, could you take me to the hospital?"

Michael: "Okay, I will drive the car around to the front door while you put on some clothes."

Shawn: "I think I will just go in my PJ's."

Michael: "Okay (grabbing his key as both of them head to the car)."

The drive to the hospital was like hearing a pin drop. I wanted so very much to ask Shawn what was going on; but, decided to wait until I reach the hospital and Shawn feeling better. We pulled up to the emergency entrance to the Fulton County Memorial Hospital. As soon as the nurse took Shawn vitals, she immediately admitted him to a room. Still in dismay, I waited patiently to find out what was happening. I saw the energy of Shawn being sucked out of him like a vacuum cleaner without an on, off switch. My nerves started to weaken when Shawn came in and out of consciousness. Finally, the doctor took me to his office and asked was I family. I told him ...no and yes.

Michael (looking at the doctor almost in tears): "I'm not blood related doctor; but, we live together and I love him very much (with a tear running down his cheek)."

Doctor Johnson: "I will need to talk to family. Do your friend, Shawn Fairchield, have any close relatives (concerned)?"

Michael: "Yes, but they live out-of-state?"

Doctor Johnson: "Well, since we don't have much time. I need for you to sign a release as provisionary next to kin because we need to take him to surgery as soon as possible."

Michael (uneasy): "Doctor, what's going on with Shawn?"

Doctor Johnson (surprised): "I'm sorry Michael; but, Shawn is a diabetic."

Michael (jumping in): "Okay, I didn't know but why surgery?"

Doctor Johnson: "His right leg has no blood flowing through it. Has he been complaining about any usual pains?"

Michael: "Yes, he does work at a club that requires a lot of performing; and sometimes when he gets home, he says he has numbness in that leg."

Doctor Johnson: "We need to work on that leg immediately."

Michael (in tears): "Doctor, do what you need to.....to keep Shawn with me."

Doctor Johnson (patting Michael on the shoulder): "I'll make sure
    he will be just fine. I will talk to you after surgery."

Michael: "That's fine."

The music over the intercom in the waiting room started
playing "My life is in your hands" by Kirk Franklin. A peace came
over Michael as he begins to phone Mr. & Mrs. Fairchield. After
speaking with Michael, The Fairchield's took the next flight into
Atlanta from Colorado. Then, Michael texts Tangy to come by the
hospital when she gets a break from work. Thirty minutes later,
Earl and Tangy entered the waiting area at the hospital.

Tangy (concerned): "Munch, are you alright?"

Michael (smiling): "Yes, now that you are here sis."

Tangy (still concerned): "Are you hungry?"

Earl (standing up): "I will go down to the cafeteria and get us all
    some lunch."

Michael: "Thanks man (relived that they both are there)."

Tangy: "So, he is in surgery now?"

Michael: "Yes."

Tangy: "It's going to be okay brother. GOD has already taken care of it. We just have to walk in it."

Michael: "Yes, I know he has his angels covering Shawn and touching Doctor Johnson's hands."

Earl (coming back from the cafeteria): "Hey guys, I have shepherd's pie and some tea (making light of the occasion)!"

Michael and Tangy: "Thanks."

It seemed like forever before surgery was over. I fell asleep and woke up again and Shawn was still in the operating room. My nerves started to become weak again; hands begins to shake, and my eyes tears up. Earl soon had to leave to get back to the youth detention center on a case that he has to argue in a couple of days. Tangy took off a week from Fulton County High School. She says that she can be here for me and Shawn, while also taking a break from counseling. Finally, Doctor Johnson comes into the surgery waiting room.

Doctor Johnson: "We've manage to keep Shawn stable through surgery; but unfortunately, we couldn't save the leg! He is going to have to use crutches until the incision from the amputation heals. I am scheduling him a check-up in six months, and also counseling with a close doctor friend of mind, Doctor Wendy Matthews. She specializes in rehabilitation after trauma. Here's her information.

Michael: "Thanks Doctor. I guess it could be worst."

Tangy: "Yes, thanks Doctor Johnson (smiling)."

Doctor Johnson: "Shawn is free to go tomorrow morning for discharge."

Michael: "Could we see him now?"

Doctor Johnson: "Yes, we put him in Room 209."

Michael: "Sis, I wonder how's he is taking it?"

Tangy: "The best way to find out is to go see."

Michael and Tangy walked into Room 209. Shawn was resting in bed looking out the second floor hospital window. Outside seemed so bland, cloudy with splashes of rain on the window ceil. Shawn turns to Michael and begins to speak.

Shawn (hurt): "I've lost my leg! I've lost my leg!"

Michael (sympathetic): "We didn't know that you were diabetic..... I'm sorry about your leg.... You will be okay."

Shawn (still hurt): "I cannot perform anymore."

Michael: "I know, I know.... (understanding Shawn's pain)."

Tangy: "Shawn, look on the good side..."

Shawn (interrupting): "What good side, sis."

Tangy (continuing): "GOD has given you another day to live life and be glad in it. The devil never wins. Soon, with a prosthetic leg, you will be able to do more. May even dance again?"

Shawn: "I guess you're right (brighten up)?"

Just then, Mr. & Mrs. Fairchield enters Room 209.

Mrs. Fairchield: "Bug, we rush right over when we heard.... Are you okay?"

Shawn (thankful): "Hi Mom and Dad, I am glad you came. Michael is a nervous wreck (chuckling)."

Michael: Hi Mr. & Mrs. Fairchield. It is always a pleasure to see you. This is my little sister, Tangy."

Tangy: "I don't know about little (being taller than her brother). It's good to finally meet you."

Mr. Fairchield: "Very pretty and tall."

Tangy (still smiling): "Thank you."

Michael: "I have a room setup for you at our home (being
welcoming)."

Mr. & Mrs. Fairchield: 'That's great... We can assist with Michael
for a few days...help him get adjusted (agreeing)."

Michael: "Awesome, I plan to stay with Shawn tonight; but, Tangy
will get you settled in?"

Mr. Fairchield (a little tired): "Sounds good, Michael (as all three
leaves)."

Shawn begins to fall asleep after an overwhelming day.
Michael pulls out his Bible while resting in the hospital recliner
and starts reading from the book of Psalm:

"O sing unto the Lord a new song; for He hath done marvelous
things: His right hand, and His holy arm, hath gotten Him the
victory" (Psalm 98:1). A change is about to take place in Michael's
life, a new song of praise. Michael becomes at peace of what that
new song will bring. For, he knows it is good. Michael closes his
Bible and sleeps.

CHAPTER TWENTY-TWO

THE TRIAL

Grandma Susie asked me was I going to the trial between Angie and Bryson. I told her that I didn't want to; but, that wouldn't be the Christian thing to do. Bryson has made many mistakes in the pass as far as my bruises and feelings; but, I didn't know he had it in him to totally go off and attempt murder. When did he lose sight with the Lord? I guess it was the same time that I was putting him before Jesus myself. I started to put on the pearl earrings that my mother left me.

Grandma Susie: "Do you want me to come too baby?"

Rachel: "Oh Mama, would you?"

Grandma Susie: "Yes baby (smiling as she slipped on her Dr. Scholl's dress shoes)!"

On the way to the courthouse, all I could think of was testifying in front of Bryson. Would he come across the stand in anger to hit me once more or would he wait until he is release if that happens?

Rachel (concerned): "Mama, what would I say?"

Grandma Susie: "The truth baby, the truth…"

Rachel (still terrified): "Mama…."

Grandma Susie: "What does the Word says…. And so the Lord restored me for my righteousness, because I am clean in his eyes. You deal faithfully with the faithful; you show integrity toward the one who has integrity. You are pure toward the pure, but toward the crooked you are tricky. You are the one who saves people who suffer, but your eyes are against the proud. You bring them down! You are my lamp, Lord; the Lord illumines my darkness" (2 Samuel 22: 25-29 CEB).

Grandma Susie: "Rachel, find your strength baby… It's right here (pointing to Rachel's heart)."

Rachel: "Mama, you always know what to say (smiling and pulling up to the courthouse)!"

Angie (meeting Rachel and Grandma Susie): "Hi Rachel."

Rachel: "Hi Angie, Are you okay? How is the twins?"

Angie: They are fine. I have a girlfriend of mine looking after them."

Rachel: "I'm sorry to hear about the apartment."

Angie (sadden): "Well, I couldn't believe it as well. Good that I got out in time enough. My friend and neighbor helped me out by breaking a window when she noticed the flames of the fire. Samantha, Kyle, and I stay with her next door."

Rachel: "You have to bring them by Mama's one weekend to visit.... This is the address and my new cell phone number (passing a business card to Angie with the new information on the back).

Angie: "Sure will...thanks."

The trial seemed like forever. The plaintiff lawyer devours Bryson's character, and claims him to be an unfit parent to continue to take full custody of the twins. In that moment, I saw tears roll down from Bryson's eyes. It seems the trial and the three month wait changed Bryson. He didn't argue on the complaints brought against him; but instead, acknowledge what he had done to Angie. Suddenly, I saw the man that I felled in-love with; but, I knew it would be seasons before we could talk again. I already called my lawyer to be counseled for divorce. Lord, am I doing the right thing? Should I give up on my marriage? I made vows for better or worse... Is this the end or a beginning? Time will bring on a change. Angie has the twins, the house, and most of our money. She has been vacationing in the islands and catching up on lost times....being broke I guess. I don't blame her. She has been through so much these past years. Now, Bryson is broke and now in jail for the next ten years. At times, I am sorry for him and at times I just want to let him suffer like I had suffered--- and eye for an eye (singing that upbeat R&B song, "Hurt You" by Toni Braxton and Babyface). Living with Grandma Susie is great. I get down home cooking, fried chicken, candy yams, flapjacks, mustard greens, and my favorite, Grandma Susie's Strawberry pound cake. Yass! Mama knows just what to do; but, I have to find my own space. Joy Denita will be coming home soon and a girl have needs (thinking about the lavender dill doe that she keeps in her top dresser drawer when she visits Grandma Susie and Bryson is nowhere to be found). I close the drawer and start citing from Psalms 71:1-3 (MSG): "I run for dear life to God, I'll never live to regret it. Do what you do so well; get me out of this mess and up on my feet. Put your ear to the ground and listen, give me space for salvation. Be a guest room where I can retreat; you said your door was always open! You're my salvation--- my vast, granite fortress."

I started my daily run and check Mama's mailbox. All I saw where creditors from both Bryson's and I joint accounts. I cannot believe with the money we had made, he spent foolishly. Now, my eight hour work day have turn into twelve hours, and sometimes overnights. Then, it dropped...the first letter from Bryson. I opened the letter and started reading:

> Hi Love,
>
> First of all I want to say that I am wrong. I apologize. I took our love for granted and foolishly done wrong by abusing what God gave us. . . . .

I stopped reading at that moment because, in the beginning, I thought Bryson truly love me and God. But after being married to his "selfish self," I realized he was a lie (in anger). Wow! How could he put God in the things he did and brought me to? He should've listen to God if he couldn't listen to me in our marriage.

Now, that I told him I am filing for divorce, he wants to renew our marriage. Wow (as she ripped the letter up without reading the entire letter)! Then, I got into Grandma Susie's old Toyota sedan for work, since my BMW got reprocessed. Damned that Bryson!

PRISON LIFE

As I sit here (humming "Clean This House" by Isaac Carree) in my cell, I think about my life and how I screwed it up. It's been eight months. I did the same thing to Rachel as Angie. The only difference is that I truly love Rachel. God, how could I be so stupid. I always had a sexual addiction; but I didn't know that would make me so angry when Rachel just didn't want to. This woman stood by me through the bruises and insecurities and shown love. I think the hospital incident and taking private trips to see Karen changed Rachel. She started fighting back. She didn't know that I saw the paperwork for a new account at Truce Bank. Yes, Rachel started taking one thousand dollars out our joint account every two weeks. Yes, I can say very smart. I got so angry that I grabbed her hair and pulled her down the stairs in rage. God definitely stepped in with my arrest because I wanted to kill her. Angie always took me there in rage among taking our money for foolish things; so, I just snapped! Yes, snapped! How can I get my life back on track? I decided to enroll in addiction classes along with my duties here as inmate 203. My first class is tomorrow. Then, I heard cell number 202 inmate, right next to me, started calling me.

202 inmate: "What's up 203? What are you in for brother (in a
    deep voice)?"
Bryson: "Why (in a tough voice)?"
Inmate 202: "I heard you like to beat on defensive women?"
Bryson: "You cannot believe everything you hear."
Inmate 202: "Things are usually very accurate around here."

Bryson: "What are you in for?"

Inmate 202: "At age eighteen, I killed my mama's second husband
    after he throw gasoline on her in a heated argument for not
    being home on time. Luckily, he couldn't find the matches
    that I threw away while I got out my dad's thirty eight. It
    never misses. I miss my dad; he was the real deal."

Bryson: "How long?"

Inmate 202: "It's been twenty-four life-changing years, from a boy to a man. I've been praying that God give me mercy and allow me to meet my twenty-four year-old son that was snatched from me years ago. Do you believe in God?"

Bryson: "Sometimes."

Inmate 202: "Why sometimes?"

Bryson: "It's complicated."

Inmate 202: "Young blood ... I have the rest of my life to hear. At least that's what these punk ass officers keep telling me."

Bryson: "My dad was a highly influential person personally as well as professionally. He molded me into the man I am today. However, I thought I would never walk into his shoes as a young man; but, I was wrong. One day, I saw him having sex with JuJu, my nanny, at the age of sixteen. I overheard mom yelling when dad told her it has been going on since she started as my nanny. Because I told mom, dad ships me to in-list into the army to provide for myself. He is dead now, a heart attack. I managed to become a millionaire before army retirement; but now I have nothing. Absolutely..... nothing. My wife is divorcing me. I have a record. And most of all, I have defiled God.

I don't know where to start in making things right. My lawyer signed me up for addiction and abuse classes to lessen my sentence; but I don't think it will help (losing his faith)."

Inmate 202: "Young blood.....read Luke chapter 12. Talk to you later (as he goes to sleep)."

Bryson (opening his Bible Rachel gave to him):

"For there is nothing covered, that shall not be revealed; neither hid, that shall not be known. Therefore, whatsoever ye have spoken in darkness shall be heard in the light; and that which ye have spoken in the ear in closets shall be proclaimed upon the housetops. And I say unto you my friends; Be not afraid of them that kill the body, and after that have no more that they can do. But I will forewarn you whom ye shall fear: Fear him, which after he hath killed hath power to cast into hell; yea, I say unto you. Fear him.... For the Holy Ghost shall teach you in the same hour what ye ought to say (Luke 12:2-5, 12 KJV)."

CHAPTER TWENTY-FOUR

PASTOR MARKS ALMOST CHEATS

Sitting here at my desk at the church can be relaxing... I don't hear Kelly's nagging in the background on what I have and have not done around the house. So what if we pay a gardener instead of me making sacrifices for the church. Nag! Nag! Nag! Being head pastor takes commitment and patience. How do we expect to expand St. John's into an accredited college for not only members, the community, but also surrounding states and eventually the country? That's the vision (while writing and brainstorming more on project S.J.U.—

Saint John's University)! My wife has been acting strange lately, eating less and coming home later. I hope she is not depressed (as he finishes up and drives home).

Pastor Marks (yelling from downstairs of his home): "Kelly, I'm home.... Kelly, I'm home (no answer)."

Pastor Marks (walking into his bedroom and seeing lingerie lying everywhere): "Kelly, what's going on (then seeing a note on the night stand)?"

Pastor Marks (reading the note from First Lady Kelly): "Marks, I will be home a little late tonight. I love you, Kelly (tearing up the note and turning in for the night in anger)."

Today was a fulfilling day! I went to Weight Watchers after work. I cannot believe that I am at a total of fifteen pounds lighter. I really don't think that Marks have notice. Why should I bother? The main reason for losing the weight is for him to notice me, and give me the encouragement to gain strength within myself and to look in the mirror and say again .... Beautiful, not disappointing. It's the way he looks at me when he does, and the way he pulls away from me when I try to get close. I truly feel deep down inside he still loves me. But, I believe it's hidden underneath the extra skin which folds within me. I carried this weight ... this weight (touching her belly and then her heart) for twenty years. God truly has explaining to do. I am a great steward, wife, and mentor to many. Then, I remember the seven most deadly sins: wrath (Proverbs 15:1), greed (Ephesians 4:19), laziness (Proverbs 15:19), pride (Proverbs 16:18), lust (Mathews 5:28), envy (1 Peter 2:1-2), and gluttony (Proverbs 23:21).

I immediately pull out my new iPhone after leaving my "me dinner" and walking to my car. Yes, I upgraded! I started taking myself out to dinner.... relearning myself. So I started treating myself once a week of what I call "me time." Rather it's "me dinner," "me spa," or just "me time;" I learnt how to not worry about what others may be thinking of me because now in a long time I feel beautiful. I started reading more on the seven deadly sins and how the depths of one can lead to another. I search the word "gluttony" and here's what I read:

The sin of gluttony is one of the most difficult of the seven deadly sins to understand. It is define as the excess of eating or drinking or a greedy or excessive indulgence. Gluttony overlaps with greed. People who sin as a glutton can have lack of discipline and would do anything to fulfill their lustful desires. For Proverbs 23:21 says, "For the drunkard and the glutton shall clothe a man with rags." Shoot! All this time I thought I indulge in food because of the lack of attention at home. Well by reading this web link, I realize I had a lustful desire to fulfill a need that only God can fulfill. By focusing on "me time" and the walk I need to take to become a better Christian, I notice I can be a better person; and thus a better wife and potential mother. The sky's the limit (as I pick up an adoption pamphlet before entering the building of "A New Start)! I cannot wait to tell Marks (smiling)!

Before coming home, Teresa Boyd, my flamboyant secretary offers the usual....a dinner with her after work. I declined. Along time ago, I had a shameful encounter with Teresa that should have never taken place. We were alone in the office doing some filing and late night church business. I knew I should have waited until the next day to finish when my secretary implanted her lips on mine. I flew to the door, leaving everything behind including my sermon notes and bible. Sometimes when you are in a bad situation, one has to flea instead of just walking out, and this was one of those times. As I reached the door, Kelly stops me. Shucks! Do you know Kelly lost her religion in that moment, and pull Teresa by the hair and drugged her out of my office? Wow! The only reason why she is still here is that she is still under contract and have too many shares in St. John's, with her granddad once being a bishop of the church. But, Kelly always keeps her in check. I guess the thought of being dragged again is a painful recap... Lol (Marks open up his desktop for the last time that evening).

Pastor Marks (reading from tomorrow's sermon notes):

Today I want to talk about having too much that we forget to appreciate what God has already done in our lives. The glutton is never satisfied and always wants more. It's very important to stay content in any situation because there is always someone who has it worse than you. God says lean not to your own understanding but in all things acknowledge Him and He will direct your paths (Proverbs 3:5-6). If we listen to people, we will feel that we are inadequate and lacking in some areas of our lives. But God says he will give us the desires of our heart if we patiently wait upon Him and only Him. Man cannot do what God can do......Again, man....cannot ....do what God can do saints..... I want to acknowledge Him and step behind the cross and say that I am inadequate when it comes to God. Yes we are imperfect people. If we look to man instead of God for deliverance, healing, or finances; we will become short because God and only Him controls it all. The Word says, we cannot get to The Father without going through the son, let's read John 14:

"I am the way, the truth, and the life: no man cometh unto the Father, but by me.... And whatsoever ye shall ask in my name, that will I do, that the Father may be glorified in the Son. If ye

shall ask any thing in my name, I will do it. If ye love me, keep my commandments. And I will pray the Father, and he shall give you another Comforter, that he may abide with you forever.....I will not leave you comfortless: I will come to you" (John 14:6, 13-16, 18). God says wait... yes wait on Him. Live each moment like it's your last... Put Jesus in your plans when implementing daily tasks... Let Him know that none of it will be possible without His favor.... And if your plans do not all come to past that day... Know that because you have His favor...it will pass in due season....Trust and believe that God has it all under control. Praise Him Now! Praise Him Now! Hallelujah!

CHAPTER TWENTY-FIVE

TANGY TESTIFIES

After teaching, I decided I wanted to pamper myself for date night with Xavier Earl. God has been so good to me. I pull up to the spa and sat down in the next available chair. Dawn Monet, the owner, always gets me the best seat since I am a valued client of hers. I had Amy today and boy she is quick but very talkative. I call her, The Message Board" because if anyone can get your business out in big town Atlanta; it would be Amy Varcelia, our Spanish-American.

Dawn (preparing a bank deposit from last night): "Hi Tangy, it's been a long time. We missed you. How does it feel to be married finally?"

Tangy: "I still cannot believe that I am ...actually! It seems surreal (smiling)!"

Dawn (winking her eyes at Tangy): "I remember a time when the girls and I begin to wonder about you (still smiling)."

Tangy: "Oh Yea, mind your own business Ms. Monet! You had enough husbands for the both of us (smiling and rolling her eyes)."

Tangy: "Amy, are you taking notes? I don't want my business in the paper tomorrow. The headliner reading, A Lesbian getting her groove back (in a warning voice and then laughing)?"

Amy (feeling insulted): "Little do you know Tangy or shall I say Mrs. Xavier Earl Gilmoore ...I have turned over a new leaf!"

Tangy: "Don't turn that leaf back over tomorrow (all the girls in the spa laughing and laughing).

Tangy: "On the real girls, I'm not going to lie. There was a point in my life that I questioned my sexuality fearing that I would never find a descent brother. You know how the devil can attempt to get into your thoughts of purity and try to convince you that you are not who God say you are...

His child. Yes, His child. Homosexuality is sin and there's no excuse for it. Although we all sin, the devil tries to take your weaknesses for own pleasures. Dawn you know better than anyone how wild I was back in undergrad, exploring men as well as women. Until one day, I picked up the Bible and begin reading and reading. Before a year was up, I had read Genesis through Revelations. Yes, I can say it wasn't easy; but through God's Word, I became whole. I had become content with where I was, successful, independent, and happy. I knew that I didn't have all the things I wanted at that moment; but, I had enough. And, I knew if God didn't do another thing in my life; He had done enough. I woke up being thankful no matter what happens and acknowledge Him in everything. That's how I came over on homosexuality and the ties it has in my family. Michael is my brother as well as my friend, and I keep praying for him. One day, I know God will answer my prayers about him also.

Dawn (smiling at Tangy while grabbing her purse): "Indeed He will! Tangy I still have him on my prayer list (exiting the building)!"

Amy: "Yes Tangy, in due season. I'm still praying too (smiling while saying this service is on the house). I love you."

The Girls at the Spa: "We love you too Tangy!"

Tangy (smiling with tears): "I love this place. Y'all just know how to treat a girl (group hugs with spa staff and then Amy cuts on the local radio)."

Pastor Mark's Night Talk Radio

Let me tell you how the devil works.....He will do anything to corrupt your soul, body, and mind. That's' his business to kill, steal, and destroy. If you are in a bad situation, I'm going to tell you how to get out...... Do you know that prayer changes things? I think I'm going to have to say this again ..... Do you know that having faith in God destroys any stronghold the devils plots against you? Faith, the belief that God do exists, angers the devil. Because he has peek into your future and saw what God has already planned for your life, the devil becomes angry. So angry, that he tries to convince you that you are not worth the blessing that is about to unfold. Let's look at 1 Chronicles 4: 9-10: "Now Jabez was more honorable than his brothers, and his mother called his name Jabez, saying, 'Because I bore him in pain.' And Jabez called on the God of Israel saying, 'Oh, that You would bless me indeed, and enlarge my territory, that

Your hand would be with me, and that You would keep me from evil, that I may not cause pain.' So God granted him what he requested.' Jabez was honorable and the Word says far more than his brothers. Why does God grant Jabez his prayer request? Because he went to God earnestly, being serious in intention, purpose, and effort; and using humility, being humbled despite the personal importance of his prayer request. God is God! He doesn't have to do another thing for us. He is faithful! Because He loves us so much, He hears even the smallest prayers...It's up to us to ask for them. As, The Word says, "Ask and it will be given to you; seek and you will find; knock and the door will be opened to you. For everyone who asks receives; the one who seeks finds; and to the one who knocks, the door will be opened" (Mathew 7: 7-8 NIV). Open your blessings today....God is waiting! Good Nite.

CHAPTER TWENTY-SIX

THE MARKS, FOSTER PARENTS?

First Lady Kelly walks into the door after another day out at Weight Watchers. She puts down her workout bag, starts dinner, and decides to confront Marks on his behavior lately and ask him to be open to foster care.

First Lady Kelly (reading from her Bible before going in the den to talk to Marks):

"Now faith is the substance of things hoped for, the evidence of things not seen (Hebrews 11:1 KJV)."

First Lady Kelly (entering into the den): "Marks Papito, I love you. I know you have been busy lately and so have I; but, we need to get back to the loving part of our marriage."

Marks (the first time really noticing Kelly in years): "Hi honey, I love you too. We have been distant for a long time. At first, I thought that it was you; but, all the while...... honey, it's been me. I have put any and everything above what's important. And, that is you.... You are my rib and love. The expansion doesn't matter and the sermon has a back seat. I want you and only you, my love!"

First Lady Kelly (glazing in Marks tearing eyes): "Babe, I am glad you see me now; and, I know we can move forward. You are a great man and leader of many, and I would be selfish not to share you (kissing his cheek)."

First Lady Kelly (still smiling): "But there is one thing I ask of you. I would love to have your child."

Marks: "Honey, I know there is so much new technology out there; and, I do believe in the story of Abraham and Sarah. But, how's that possible (in confusion because of their ages)?"

First Lady Kelly: "With God. It's funny how life gives you curve balls. If we would have it our way we would have things we want when we want them. Shucks! Nobody wants to wait for our hearts most desires. However, patience is Love. God throws curve balls, not to discourage us; but, for us to find a different route in hitting them. Life is difficult at times; but through patience and faith….this too shall pass. Let's find the things that make us HaPpy and let's live in this moment. Marks, let's adopt."

Marks (smiling and then laughing): "Yes honey, let's adopt (kissing Kelly the same as when he thought of her back when as Miss Firecracker)!"

Suddenly, the lights in the Marks' home fade away.

CHAPTER TWENTY-SEVEN

HIS Plans, Not Mine

Shawn hasn't been doing very well lately. I can see the pain in his eyes as he does home therapy with hospital staff. Shawn's leg was his pride and joy; letting him transform into any dance character he wanted at that given moment. Although, he still has one and his prosthetic leg is coming tomorrow. He still has pain not only in his leg, but also his heart. I pray every day for him; but, God keeps telling me to prepare for a change. I don't know what that change may be; but I know it's coming soon because it cannot get any worse. All of a sudden Shawn begins to tremble. The physical therapist says he's having a sugar attack..... and then shouts hurry let's get him to a doctor. Shawn starts to turn blue-black with signs of no oxygen in his face. It took the ambulance ten minutes to transfer Shawn from the therapy extension building to the main hospital, the buildings were located on different streets, where therapy staff commutes daily.

I hopped into my dependable Toyota Camry and drove behind the ambulance. Then, I saw the ambulance stop. We were at the emergency entrance; but the EMT's had slowed.....Lady Bug was gone. Lady Bug was gone...and so was my friend.... "my" friend! The staff said they tried to resuscitate; but it was unsuccessful. I stopped, dropped, and fell to my knees. At that moment, I begin to question God. Then, I thought about Job, a faithful man, who didn't curse God after so much pain. Job's physical well-being was destroyed so his spiritual being could manifest itself to be a testimony to others. Job was not perfect, but in his lowest moment....he did not curse God. In that next moment, I started to praise Jesus for what He was preparing me for. Then, I heard a voice, one of the hospital EMT's.

EMT Staff: "Hi, it's going to be just fine (smiling)."
Michael (turning around): "Hi, thank you (the last tears falling from his eyes).
EMT Staff: "I'm Tiffany Livingston (pulling out her hand to shake with Michael).

Michael (softly grasping her hand): "I know....he's free now...from the pain, the pain of living without his leg. Shawn now can dance for Jesus. If Jesus loved the woman with the issue of blood, I know he would love Michael, my friend."

Tiffany: "Yes, He will. Shawn faith is strong. He cried out forgiveness to Jesus before passing and look into my eyes and told me...go to Michael. He repeated...go to Michael and then he surrendered. We tried to bring him back.... God knows best."

Michael: "Thank you."

Tiffany: "You're welcomed."

As Tiffany walked pass Michael, he begin to notice the sweetness of Tiffany's perfume. He looked at her walk away and smiled. I went home and open the good book. I begin reading from Job 2: 3-10:

"And the Lord said unto Satan, Hast thou considered my servant Job, that there is none like him in the earth, a perfect and an upright man, one that feareth God and escheweth evil? And still he holdeth fast his integrity, although thou movedst me against him, to destroy him without cause. And Satan answered the Lord, and said skin for skin, yea, all that a man hath will he give for his life. But put forth thine hand now, and touch his bone and his flesh, and he will curse thee to thy face. And the Lord said unto Satan, Behold, he is in thine hand; but save his life. So went Satan forth from the presence of the Lord, and smote Job with sore boils from the sole of his foot unto his crown. And he took him a potsherd to scrape himself withal; and he sat down among the ashes. Then said his wife unto him, Dost thou still retain thine integrity? Curse God, and die. But he said unto her, Thou speakest as one of the foolish women speaketh. What? Shall we receive good at the hand of God, and shall we not receive evil? In all, this did not Job sin with his lips" (Job 2: 3-10 KJV). Michael closes his Bible and sleeps.

The next morning, Michael decides to sing a new song. All he could think of was Jesus. He started a new routine to his life: work, exercise, and prayer. He work so he could maintain his stability at home. Michael exercise to become stronger in faith; and he continues to pray so he wouldn't lose sight for Whom is his direction. Shawn wanted to be cremated. So, Mr. and Mrs. Fairchield honored his wishes and his remains where poured over the Pacific Ocean, which was also Shawn's request. I begin packing his belongings and shipped them to the Fairchield's. I kept nothing but the memory of Shawn's laugh. Still today, that's what I remember.....his laugh.

One day I was jogging near Fulton Memorial Hospital and I saw Miss Tiffany Livingston. I approached her and begin a conversation.

Michael (looking at her bouncing curly blonde hair as she walks towards him): "Hi Tiffany. I didn't know you exercise around here."

Tiffany: "Yes, every Monday, Wednesday, and Friday (smiling)."

Michael: "How long have you been working out. You look great!"

Tiffany: "A while now (with a small giggle)."

Michael: "Would you like to work-out sometimes since we are both here during this time in the mornings?"

Tiffany: "That would be great Michael (still smiling)."

Michael: "Meet you here the same time Wednesday?"

Tiffany: "See you then (starting to walk to her car after looking at her watch). Talk to you soon. My boss gets mad when I get to work late."

Michael: "Okay...looking forward to seeing you again Tiffany."

Tiffany green eyes begin to sparkle as she drives away.

CHAPTER TWENTY-EIGHT

RACHEL DECIDES TO MOVE TO OLD HOUSE

I have been with Grandma Susie for some time now. I managed to save enough money to get most of Bryson's and I joint bills under control. Bryson still don't know about Denita Joy. The baby ward of the Fulton County Memorial says that I can bring my little girl home....finally home. I didn't want to bring the burden to Grandma Susie with a baby crying late nights; although, she says she wouldn't have it no other way. I learnt that at some point you need to leave when someone says you can stay with them. Besides, you wouldn't want to warm out your welcome. Grandma Susie is the only family I have that cares so I don't want to put a wedge in-between us. I think back when Bryson and I were swinging at the Brobaski's. I look down at Denita Joy as her baby blue eyes smiles at me. Grandma Susie is one-half Cherokee Indian with deep grey eyes....but where this curly red hair come from? Lord, I hope this child isn't his's.....no not his's... (thinking about her unforgettable past). At last, I have the studio to myself. I change it so I would have inspiration for my Gospel album. I look down at Denita Joy and said inspiration enough and kiss her cheeks filled with breast milk. I open the piano and begin singing:

Lord, prepare me to be a sanctuary, pure and holy, tried and true

And with thanksgiving, I'll be a living, sanctuary oh for you

Lord, prepare me to be a sanctuary, pure and holy, tried and true

And with thanksgiving, I'll be a living, sanctuary oh for you

After finishing the old hymn to my new song, I decided to lay Denita Joy down for a nap and check the mailbox. I am so happy. Angie decided to sell me back the house. She says she has no use for it. The twins are getting bigger (as I look at the pictures she put in a letter addressed to me). Then, I notice it.....another letter from Bryson. I decided to read it:

Hey Love,

I writing you again because I realize that you probably trash all other letters. I hope this one reaches you Rachel. Again, I want to say that I am sorry....truly sorry.

I love you, Bryson.

I decided to put that letter in a keepsake box and all other letters Bryson sends. I have a change of heart. If God can forgive us, why can't I forgive my husband? I also contacted my lawyer to postpone all further paperwork for divorce until later notice. That gave me peace....peace. I took vows with Bryson for better or worse, and I am not the type of wife to give up so easily. Yes, I can say this is the "ugly" in the good, bad, and ugly; but, that's my commitment to God as well as my husband. If it is said that the third chord in the "three-stringed chord" is God and because favor was still on our marriage; His love will pull us through. I check on Denita Joy who was still sound asleep, begin to unpack our things, and later started redecorating our home with love. Then, I pick up the phone to call Uncle Earl. I haven't spoken to him since the trial.

Rachel: "Hello Auntie, is Uncle Earl available?"

Tangy: "Yes, he's outside mowing grass. But, hold on for a minute. I'll go get him."

Uncle Earl: "Hi niece. I been awaiting your call. Bryson says he's been trying to reach you. Rachel baby, he is really sorry. He told me everything about the fights."

Rachel (missing Bryson): "I know."

Rachel: "Uncle Earl, how do you and Auntie manage to keep the love you have for each other?"

Uncle Earl: "Prayer. It isn't easy always and we had backtracks. Marriage has its good and bad times. Always emphasize the positive, and when the bad comes the key is to never give up or in. Things will get better with time niece."

Rachel: "Thanks Uncle. I love y'all and congrats on the baby."

Uncle Earl: "Yes, it a miracle and Tangy and I are so blessed."

Uncle Earl (smiling): "Did you know that God specializes in the impossible?"

Rachel: "I'm realizing this every day. Good-bye Uncle Earl."

Uncle Earl: "Bye niece (while hanging up the phone)."

GRANDMA SUSIE'S WAR

Lord, I knew that it was going to happen; but I just didn't know when. I have been fighting this battle for some time now. Jesus, I feel that I don't have anything left. This is my time. I decided not to do anymore chemo. I have prepared myself for this (as I look at the hospice resort brochure near the mountains that I sent in the last payment for last month). Rachel will be devastated to know that I am leaving her, so I left a letter address to her to explain why it's time. I place the letter in the mail while I take a taxi to the nearest airport to go to my destination, Colorado.

As I enter the airport, all I could hear is the sound of airplanes pulling in and out, like the winds trying to whisper to me. I pull out "old faithful" and begin reading Revelation 21:

"And I saw a new heaven and a new earth: for the first heaven and the first earth were passed away; and there was no more sea.... And I heard a great voice out of heaven saying, Behold, the tabernacle of God is with me, and he will dwell with them, and they shall be his people, and God himself shall be with them, and be their God....And God shall wipe away all tears from their eyes; and there shall be no more death, neither sorrow, nor crying, neither shall there be any more pain: for the former things are passed away" (Revelation 21: 1,3-4).

I close my Bible and went to sleep as I traveled to my next destination.

TIRED OF RUNNING.

When I heard that the police had picked Bryson up and took him to jail, Karen and I fled and have been running ever since. Karen stayed with me from city to city and hotel to hotel until one day she saw me talking to another woman at a truck stop. In that moment, I tried to convince her that she is all I need now. But when I came back from taking a leak; she was gone as well as the last ten thousand we had spared from when we left Atlanta that late night without being able to get the rest out of our bank account. I manage to have three hundred stored in my socks to get by for a while. I didn't go to find her. What's the use? She will only slow me down. I felt I was better off running without her. I ran until I'd found myself on the Pacific coast at a little beach community. I decided this is where I will stay low-key for a spell. On top of all that, I was tired and hungry and needed to rest. Bryson doesn't know that I reported him as the reason for prescription meds being lost at my practice .....and me.....innocent me.... was not attached. I heard he is still fighting the sentence extension with addiction classes..... What a waste! What a waste! He always had somewhat of a soft spot.

I have been traveling for years now and now finally found a place I can call home again. I met someone who changed my life......yes my life.....for the good. His name is Bishop Chung, he is Chinese as well as Baptist. He saved me. I was drunk, high, and death was awaiting me and telling me that if I wanted to be fully free; I needed to jump....jump off that cliff and leave what I've done in this life behind and be with my father. Bishop Chung saved me by pulling me off that cliff that day with these words:

"Son, Jesus told me to tell you that he will give you grace and mercy if only you believe....if only you believe that at this moment in your life you can do what's right and live.....live the life He gave you and that you have been forgiven. You just need to forgive yourself."

I started to cry out the words....have mercy on me Lord..... have mercy on me.....your fallen son. I begin confession with the story about my father. My father wasn't a good man. He use to beat my mom badly everyday as I can remember, especially after drinking with his fellow army friends. I would secretly watch my mom wash the blood from her face as she reapply her makeup. Then, he would scorn me for all the things I didn't do quite right that day. My father just past years ago....but I carry his spirit with me. Mom is still living with the guilt of shame as well as alzheimer's in a nursing home in Georgia. I married a lady that doesn't love me. I turned her into a woman she didn't want to become. I tainted not only myself but others around me. I seem to never get it right. I studied medicine, but after a while, medicine became my allied to what was happening around me. Can Jesus forgive me........"A dirty sinner?" My hands haven't been clean in a long time. Bishop Chung steps in and ask when I remember in my heart that I had lost my way.

Mom used to read the Bible to me. Until one day, dad found out and took that away from us......actually threw the Bible in the fireplace out of anger after drinking and said he doesn't want to see this in his house again...... He was an atheist...a non-believer. Bishop Chung intervenes..... Son, no one can take God from you because He lives in all of us good or bad. When He made us, He made us in His likeness so we can be like Him. Although in this life, we will always be imperfect, we have the innate desire to be just like him....and son... you are no different.

I want to be your mentor. In the next days of your life, you will learn again how to pray, love, and worship God. My church is three blocks from here. Meet me there five o'clock sharp tomorrow morning. I arrived the next day to the local church by the beach. The first day I just listen to others testimonies after our group yoga classes. One guy came to Christ after committing murder of his family after being so high one day out of rage. Bishop Chung specializes in the most overlooked sinners, and pulls the light in them out of all the dark things they keep inside. Another woman live her early life as a whore in this same community. She is now Bishop Chung's assistant minister. Minister Lara Redd brings more and more women to the church through the church's women ministries for abused and battered women.

After so many months, I brought a beach house with the intentions of bringing mom here to live with me. I withdraw the rest out of the account at a nearby location, but was very surprise to see it haven't been touch for this long. I also saved good money through the pharmacy I opened that is connected to my home. I've found how to use the gift God gave me and put it to us in a positive light. That light illuminates sight and hope for my patients as well as me through my Christian-based facility.

I started citing a message of mine when I learnt of a fellow church member confining in me about the difficulties on his job. He cried out that he is in total despair and sadness. He has been working at his job for years now, and do blue collar work as a security officer. Management at the factory he works at are looking at him to move up the last five years before retirement to train others on the importance of safety, loyalty, as well as, production. He said he took the job.... But stress, no sleep, and heartaches followed. He don't see his daughters and wife much. And now, the same management is threatening to fire him without retirement benefits; if he doesn't keep up with the extra work hours. He regrets the decision he made..... Two kids in college....twins and double the costs. But, there's no point of return now. His family cannot live without his retirement. And on top of all this, his health is fading.....a bad kidney. I fell to my knees and started to intercede on my fellow church friend. I yelled out while listening to Tamela Mann's CD.....

"Lord, take me to the King! I need your help.....help to strengthen my friend. It's too much war among our brothers and sisters....negativity inside is showing on the outside. Show us Lord that your yoke is easy and you make our burdens light.... For, you are God of all and holds it all.....Jesus....bring out the good in me and others and let your presence be known...Emmanuel! Emmanuel!

A couple of days later, I went in to work as usually and guess who I saw, my friend, a security officer. He looked really bad and it looked like he had been weeping. I knew something was terribly wrong because men just don't cry easily.

Roy (concerned): "Hi Thomas! What's going on man (somewhat afraid to ask)?"

Thomas: "It's gone.....It's gone."

Roy: "What man.....what's gone?"
Thomas: "All that I've worked for.....my job....years of hard work, dedication, and loyalty. I couldn't go home because we don't have one anymore...."

Roy: "Why do you say that?"

Thomas: "My medical bills have been so heavy financially lately; we're behind several payments on our home and no means to re-finance again because of my credit."

Roy (not knowing what to say): "Wow, sorry to hear that man! But, there's always a ram in the bush. Because you have Jesus on your side, there's a plan.....We just have to walk in it."

Thomas (smiling): "Thanks man. I needed that."

Roy: "You know man. I can use some help around here. I need someone to manage things when I can't be here. Would that be something you might be interested in?"

Thomas: "Like you say....There's always a ram in the bush (Lol)."

Roy: "See you tomorrow around seven sharp?"

Thomas: "Tomorrow.... (while walking out the door praising God for his blessing)."

I closed the pharmacy that night listening to Vicki Yohe's song on the intercom, "Deliverance is Available," while thinking about my wife, Karen, and friend, Bryson. I knew I had some unfinished business to take care of and knew now was the time to face it. Thomas came in the next few days and I trained him to run the pharmacy while I was gone. Shelia, my assistant pharmacist tech, helped out also. Shelia is a single mom who is now turned lesbian. Shelia married her wife after a very abusive first marriage. Her wife is very friendly and we go to the same church. I wish things were different for her.....but she seem so very happy. I packed my bags and got on the next available flight to Atlanta. When I arrived, I tuned in to the local radio in my rental truck. I heard Pastor Marks on the air speaking on the recorded sermon from last Sunday:

Pastor Marks Radio Broadcast
Message: Don't Judge Me! If you haven't been through it, you don't know.

The Bible says there is nothing new under the sun (Ecclesiastes 1:9). In this life, you will be tested....tested through you family, friends, work, church home, and then your faith. In our wrongdoings...the devil will try to convince us that we don't have a purpose......that we are useless human-beings not able to please God. Then, we start to believe the negative things that people say about us.....and engrave it into our spirits...... Soon, we start doing the same things to others. Jealousy, Envy, Greed, Pride, Lust, Anger, and Gluttony is not things of today but that of yesterday also. In order to understand totally what a person is going through, we had to have gone through it ourselves. ...... A repeated idea of today is judging others...... We judge because we cannot truly understand what someone is going through..... Rather than judge, Christians should empathize..... empathize with the purest of heart and understand the basis of cause that made the effect ...... say nothing if necessary...Saying nothing and listening can also be very powerful.... Like the old folks say, "if you don't have nothing good to say....say nothing at all." The tongue is the most powerful instrument in us today..... The tongue can try to destroy a person heart, mind, and even character..... But, one thing the tongue cannot do....It cannot destroy a person's soul if it's with God. Church, let's walk in the likeness of Jesus Christ and cloth and shelter the homeless, feed the hungry, listen to our children, be a friend to the whoremonger and drunkard, and most importantly love the fallen sinner. Let's see the good in all people because there's good in every human-being. God brings us through things to be a testimony to others.....Your testimony is so powerful that only if you went through it yourself can the full manifestation of His power come through to that fallen sinner....How can we judge when we are still being cleaned......Again, how can we give advice when we haven't been through it..... Daily, we need to ask the Holy Spirit for cleanliness..... For, the Word says if you pray to the Father,

he will give you a Comforter to abide with you forever (John 14:16)
who can direct our paths ....and goes on to say that in the way
you judge others, you will be judged the same (Matthew7: 1-2). In
closing, let God be the judge.....He and Only He.....can change people
for the good.....It's our job to bring the Good News.....The Good News
that Jesus loves us despite our inconsistencies or discrepancies.... so
might others come to Him.....in truth and in life. Let go of our pride,
greed, lust, jealousy, anger, or gluttony and love to be loved. The
kingdom of Jesus Christ is waiting....

Then, the song, "I almost let go" by Kurt Carr filled my new rental truck. I smiled and headed to the old neighborhood.

CHAPTER THIRTY-ONE

KAREN'S BACK

I ran and ran with Roy until I couldn't run anymore. I saw Roy with another woman for the last time. Eye for an eye doesn't always return in your favor; but only gives you temporary satisfaction. I knew it was enough. I decided long time ago, to stop trying to please my worthless husband. He blackmailed me as well as threatened me with our money if at any time I decided to leave him. That's why I left it.....I left the money. Before, I got use to our extra-curriculum activities..... flip flopping from one thing to the next. Pleasing him was impossible. I guess this what made us gluttons.....never satisfied and always searching for more. So, I started seeing other men out of hurt, including Bryson. It was something about the way he kissed Rachel that made me curious. It was a one night thing. Although, I believe Rachel thought it was more. Bryson became a good friend to me ....coming over every day. He showed me again that I was beautiful. It's funny how sometime we can feel the grass greener on the other side. Now, that I think about it....That's the enemy plotting destruction in our lives. I begin to want more in life. I ran with Roy afraid that I would be an accomplice to sending Bryson to jail....but, I cannot run any longer. My feet are tired.

I use the money that I took from Roy for a new start, a new start to finally taking care of myself by myself. And, yes this is a good feeling! I rented an apartment close by Atlanta in the mountains. I always loved the mountains. It's time to make things right with Rachel. I decided to call her.

Karen (as Rachel's ringback tone One Moment by Vicki Yohe plays and then her voicemail picks up): "Hi Rachel. It's Karen Brobaski. I want to say that I am truly sorry to hear about Bryson.....Call me (while hanging up)?"

I wanted to say more, but thought it would be better to talk face to face. Maybe, she will have it on her heart to call back.

CHAPTER THIRTY-TWO

A RAM IN THE BUSH

Marks and I have been doing great lately. We've found the loving part of our relationship back. I feel more confident because I decided to change what I didn't like about myself. Now I have dropped four pant sizes, I am a size sixteen with the mindset of a ten. Yes, I did that! I am healthy, happy, and in-love again. Marks make time for us now and our family comes first in his life. We have taken all our classes for foster care; but, it's been months now and haven't got placement. I tried contacting the agency, but was told that everything is still in-process. I started to question rather this will come to pass.

Early one Sunday morning, Marks and I decided to get to the church early to pray for direction. All of sudden, the door of Marks office opened. It was a teenager who seems to be hungry and endangered as she devours a piece of apple she sold from a nearby fruit stand. I hear the worker outside saying catch her ....thief....She ran in and asks to wait here for a spell. Marks hear another man calling Angel, Angel....I know you are here.... come on I have something special for you. And then, he left and got back into his automobile and sprinted off. He pulls off so fast, a cop watching him nearby came chasing after him. Then, the young woman started thanking God that this may buy her sometime.

First Lady Kelly: "Hi honey, are you okay?"

Angel (still a little nervous and on edge shaking): "I think so."

First Lady Kelly: "Why are you running child? Are you in trouble?"

Angel (smiling): "A little (while pointing at her stomach."

Pastor Marks (pulling Kelly to the side): "Babe....Why don't we allow her to stay with us just until she is more settled?"

First Lady Kelly: "Okay honey....yes, I think that would be best. I don't want her back where she came from."

First Lady Kelly: "Suga, I am Kelly and this is Pastor Marks. We want you to stay with us for a while until we can make other arrangements. Is that okay with you?"

Angel (still smiling): "Thank you so much. I believe that would be just fine (while rubbing her protruding tummy)."

The Marks welcomed Angel into their home and told her she can stay until something better comes along for her and Pink. This is the name Angel calls her as she rubs her stomach. The Marks knows this is a blessing. Not only do they get the chance to love Angel; but also here unborn little girl. They are expecting a baby real soon. God is still good! First Lady Kelly decides to take Angel to the doctor. Angel was a little hesitant at first because she knew roaming the streets and that life may have damper Pink's health. However, she explains to First Lady Kelly that the guy she seen can also be controlling to whatever he wants.

Angel (putting on her jacket): "I'm ready and I think I have everything (while putting her identification in her wallet)."

First Lady Kelly: "Okay.....coming. Marks we are gone (yelling into the study)!"

Marks (while writing next Sunday sermon): "Okay.....call me and
let me know what the doctor says."

Pastor Marks begin typing out his notes and reading aloud:

Message: A Ram in the Bush

Remember saints that God doesn't make mistakes. In the
depths of our doubts, fears, and misfortunes....God has it all under
control. When we pray...don't be surprise that you get exactly
what you've prayed for...so make sure you be specific with Him.
If you pray for a new house, car, or a better job.....be prepared.....
again I say be prepared. That house has a mortgage and the car
have payments, and that job may have more headaches.....So
saints again be specific. But......But....when that bill, payment, or
stress comes, God always has a ram in the bush. He doesn't put
us in any situation that we don't have the tools or capability to
overcome. It's in the power of calling his name.....Jesus.....Jesus....
Sweet Jesus. When we call his name demons trembles, bills get
paid, and blessings begin to unfold. Yes, there is something about
that name. Again, what's for you is for you and what's not is not.....
It might be a good season but then again you may be having a
drought....But, just remember trouble don't last always...There

is sunshine coming ahead....the forecast is in your favor....Dry those tears, put that smile on your face and remember you are loved because He loves us first.

Pastor Marks closes his desktop and begin rejoicing because he knows that Angel and Pink is home......At that moment, God gives Pastor Marks and Kelly confirmation on their prayers. Hallelujah!

Suddenly, the house phone rings. It is Kelly. The girls are fine she tells Marks. She also says that she wants Angel to stay and Marks agrees.

CHAPTER THIRTY-THREE

FLIP FLOPPERS, DO YOU KNOW HIM?

Rachel is at a great place! Her upcoming Gospel Album is in the works with a three Grammy-winning producer named, Rocks. Mama Susie is now in a better place. Rachel was able to talk with her before going home to glory. Bryson is released from prison under strict probation; and he and Rachel are mending differences while living together and working on their marriage. Michael misses Shawn but have found a new, spiritual friend in Miss Tiffany Livingston. He decides to meet Rachel and Bryson at next Sunday service at St. John's. Karen was able to talk with Rachel and have been close ever since. Rachel invites Karen to service also.

When entering the sanctuary that Sunday morning, it was purpose fulfilled. Bryson turns to his right when going towards the choir stand and sees Roy. Roy's eyes begin to water and he nods to Bryson in indication of being sorry. Karen walks in and sees Roy and sits next to him. Karen realizes that marriage is a promise to God for better or worse through rich and poor; and she still loves Roy. Michael feels little jitters when walking in the wooden-double doors. But, when he hears his sister say.....sit over here Munch; he begins to feel at home....next to Tangy and Xavier Earl. Pastor Marks look at the front pew, and sees First Lady Kelly and his adopted daughter and granddaughter Angel and Pink. He smiles and begin to speak....speak the message:

There are many temptations of this world; but, love conquers all odds. Faith is the belief that God do exists and can handle any situation or valley in life's troubles. For the good book says, "There hath not temptation taken you but such as is common to man; but God is faithful, who will not suffer you to be tempted above that ye are able; but will with the temptation also make a way to escape, that ye may be able to bear it" (1 Corinthians 10:13).

> *Faith is the belief that God do exists and can handle any situation or valley in life's troubles*

Flip Floppers are all around, individuals who flip and flops from one concept to another trying to find themselves and be accepted in the world of today. Finding oneself is through the love and salvation of the Lord. Pastor Marks emphasizes that sometimes you have to stand alone.....and continues to say......GOD has a way of doing things differently than man. He loves us despite of our sins and inconsistencies. Even when the church says no, GOD still says yes. The church is filled with imperfect individuals with humbled hearts who worship to become more like Him. The meditation of the prior is GOD intervening, making our imperfections to perfection in His eyes so that one good day we all can come be with Him. His love never fails. That's why it's important to continue to worship and praise Him in amid of ours storms and dry seasons. Being a Christian is a marriage, it has its hills and valleys and sometimes we go astray and come back to repentance; but, Jesus stays constant—He was good before and is still good now. If you are not save, turn to Him and begin a new chapter of your life with this scripture, "That if thou shalt confess with thy mouth the Lord Jesus, and shalt believe in thine heart that GOD hath raised him from the dead, thou shalt be saved (Romans 10:9 KJV)."…. Pastor Marks engages visitors and members by the words.....Welcomed! Welcomed! .....letting them know He is asking them to come. Then the St. John's Baptist Choir with Bryson as the lead begins to sing "Simply Redeemed" by Isaac

Carree. Pastor Marks open his arms stretched to embrace all who are lost to come …..The entire congregation comes to the altar and one-fourth of the congregation became saved or rededicated their lives over to Him, including Rachel, Bryson, Michael, and Karen, and Roy. GOD is still good!

"And they shall teach no more every man his neighbor, and every man his brother, saying, Know the Lord: for they shall all know me, from the least of them unto the greatest of them, saith the Lord: for I will forgive their iniquity, and I will remember their sin no more" (Jeremiah 31:34 KJV).

Special Thanks

"Lord, you are my cornerstone to which I am built.... You are the map to any situation...You are a problem solver....It is impossible to not hear you because you gave me the key...... The Holy Bible... that rests with me....Give me strength in times of trouble... Emmanuel.

-shanae m gamble

"For I know the thoughts that I think toward you, saith the Lord, thoughts of peace, and not of evil to give you a future and a hope. Then you will call upon Me and go and pray to Me, and I will listen to you. And you will seek Me and find Me, when you search for Me with all your heart" (Jeremiah 29: 11-13 KJV, The Mailbox Club, 2012)

A Special Thank You, "The Mailbox Club (Valdosta, GA)," for providing spiritual guidance and support!

-CMF

SHANAE M. GAMBLE

Shanae Gamble is an innovational writer, welcoming Christian Myths and Fables (CMF). Gamble style of writing captures her audience while aligning profound Christian ideas. Ms. Gamble has an unique way of spreading the Good News, in hopes of bringing more people to Christ. Gamble has a BBA in Marketing and a MBA in General Management with two years educational experience in Management and Psychology at the doctoral level. She has been writing since a very young age and throughout colleague years. Gamble published her first books in 2010 and again in 2011 with Christian books, The Earache Myth and GOD's dogs go to Heaven. Gamble wants the readers to engage in the stories while applying them to their lives.

"I write, therefore I am heard." © 2010

"Faith is simple, the belief that GOD do exists." © 2011

"Love conquers all odds." © 2011

"Abased by circumstances, but abound by Love." © 2015

"God's Word is the true source of comfort." © 2015

"Walls bond us from deliverance." © 2015

Christian Myths and Fables – CMF

Follow Me on Facebook @ www.facebook.
com/shanae.gamble, search Christian Myths
and Fables

Twitter Me @ Myths_Fables

Become a CMF Fan @ www.shanaegamble.
webs.com, search Guestbook

Printed in the United States
By Bookmasters